THE WHEATON BOOK OF
Myths and Legends

David Oakden

Illustrated by Peter Stevenson

Wheaton
A Division of Pergamon Press

A. Wheaton & Company Limited
A Division of Pergamon Press
Hennock Road, Exeter EX2 8RP

Pergamon Press Ltd
Headington Hill Hall, Oxford OX3 0BW

Pergamon Press Inc.
Maxwell House, Fairview Park, Elmsford, New York 10523

Pergamon of Canada Ltd
75 The East Mall, Toronto, Ontario M8Z 2L9

Pergamon Press (Australia) Pty Ltd
P.O. Box 544, Potts Point, N.S.W. 2011

Pergamon Press GmbH
6242 Kronberg/Taunus, Pferdstrasse 1, Frankfurt-am-Main,
Federal Republic of Germany

First published as three books (*Classical and Northern Stories*; *Stories from the East*; *Stories from the West*) 1978
This edition first published 1979

Printed in Great Britain by A. Wheaton & Co. Ltd, Exeter
ISBN 0 08 021436 3

CONTENTS

The Firebird

A long time ago when summers were longer and hotter than they are now, and winters were really winters, there lived in a corner of the world an old Tsar who had three sons, Dimitry, Vasily and Ivan. This old Tsar lived in a fine palace which had high walls to keep out the bitter winter winds, and a cool garden in which to laze away the sunny days. Close to one of its hundred fountains there grew a very special tree, a tree which bore every year exactly ninety-nine golden apples, and the old Tsar loved this tree better than any of his other possessions.

He was therefore extremely annoyed one morning, when he strolled out in his slippers to count the apples, to find that a whole branch had been broken off in the night, and nine apples had gone. He called his three sons to him and told them that they must take it in turns to watch over his precious tree each night from then on.

On the first night Dimitry the eldest son watched, but sad to say he fell asleep, and the next morning another branch was broken and nine more apples had gone. The next night Vasily the second son watched, but sad to say he too fell asleep and in the morning yet another branch was broken and nine more apples had gone. On the third night it was the turn of the youngest son, Ivan, to watch. Hardly had he settled his back against the smooth bark of the apple tree when there was a blinding light and there, perching in his father's favourite tree, was a beautiful firebird. Quick as a flash Ivan leapt to his feet and grabbed at the bird but, although he managed to catch it by the tail, it tore itself free and left Ivan clutching just one golden feather in his hand.

"What!" said the old Tsar the next morning, as he turned the feather round and round in his hand and stroked its golden beauty, "I must have this firebird for myself. Go, my sons, and fetch me the bird. Half of my kingdom to him who succeeds!"

Off rode Dimitry to the North, and off galloped Vasily to the South, but young Ivan mounted his horse and rode off towards the setting sun for its colours reminded him of the golden feathers of the beautiful firebird.

Ivan had not gone far when he saw a large notice which warned him that if he turned left he would certainly be eaten by wolves, while his horse would be left alone; on the other hand if he turned right his horse would be eaten and he would be left alive. Much as he loved his horse, he shrugged his shoulders and turned right, whereupon, almost immediately, his horse was attacked by a grey wolf of a huge size. Ivan jumped off and hid behind a tree, but to his amazement, as soon as the ferocious beast had eaten the horse down to its last fetlock, it came up to him and bowed low.

"Prince Ivan," said the wolf in a gruff voice, "my apologies for eating your horse, but such is the way of wolves."

"Please don't mention it," said Ivan, always polite. "But now that you have eaten my horse how am I going to find the firebird?"

"Why," said the wolf, bowing again, "that's easy enough. If you care to sit on my back I will take you to the palace of King Dolmat where the firebird sings a delightful tune in a golden cage."

So Ivan scrambled on to the bristly grey back and off they went like the wind through the black trees until they came to a gate made of brass. Through the bars Ivan could see the firebird, whistling soulfully in a high-domed golden cage.

"Now's your chance, my Prince," said the wolf, pushing the brass gate open with his long snout. "Open the cage,

2

lift out the bird and off we'll go. But whatever you do don't try to bring the cage as well, or there will be trouble."

Now whether Ivan didn't hear, or whether the wind carried away the wolf's warning, or whether he just got a bit greedy, is not known, but once he had the firebird in his hand he thought he might as well have the golden cage, and grabbed it. But it was connected by slender threads to a hundred silver alarm bells, and there appeared thirty-three spearsmen to drag him in front of King Dolmat.

King Dolmat was lean and scraggy and decidedly dirty. As he looked at Ivan and listened to his story he scratched himself and poked himself and rubbed his bristly chin with greasy fingers.

"Well, well, well," he grunted. "If only you had asked I would have given you the bird, but since you are a thief I must make you pay. Either you go and steal the horse with the golden mane from King Afran or I shall tell the whole world that I caught a son of the old Tsar stealing from my garden. You'll steal the horse? Good, I thought you might. Off you go then." And he fell to picking his nails with a broken dagger.

Ivan didn't know what to do, but luckily for him his friend the grey wolf did. Like the west wind they went, through the black trees, until they came to the palace of King Afran, and a gate of pure gold. Peering through the golden bars, Ivan could just see the glittering mane of the horse as it stamped about in a stable.

"Now's your chance, my Prince," said the wolf. "Fetch the horse, but whatever you do, don't touch its golden bridle. Quickly now, go!"

Ivan ran into the stable, caught the horse by the mane and took it out; but as he got to the door he thought it a shame to leave the bridle behind him so he reached up to lift it from its hook on the wall. But it was connected by slender threads to a hundred golden alarm bells, and sixty-six

3

swordsmen appeared to drag him in front of King Afran.

King Afran was small and incredibly pink, as though he spent all day washing and scrubbing himself. Holding a posy of flowers to his nose he said, "Well, well, well, look who we've caught stealing our golden horse. If only you had asked I would have given him to you, but now I shall have to make you pay. Either you go and fetch me the Princess Helen to be my bride or I shall tell the whole world that I caught a son of the old Tsar stealing from my stable. You'll fetch me the Princess? Good, I thought you might." And he dipped his fingers into rose-water and carefully licked each little nail.

Ivan didn't know what to do, but again his friend the grey wolf did. As swift as the west wind they rode, through the black trees, until they came to the palace of King Boris and a gate made of pure silver. Peering through the bars Ivan could see the beautiful Princess Helen sitting in the garden.

"This time," said the grey wolf, "I will do the stealing. King Boris has ninety-nine axemen who would have you cut into collops before you got through the gate."

Pushing open the gate with his black muzzle the wolf flew into the garden, seized the Princess between his jaws, flung her on to his back and was out of the garden before any of the axemen had had time to blink. Outside he stopped, Ivan jumped up behind the Princess and with a noise like the wind in the tree-tops they were gone.

Swiftly as the wolf ran, he didn't run quickly enough to prevent Ivan from falling in love with the beautiful Princess Helen, and before they reached the golden gates of King Afran he was pleading with the wolf not to make him hand her over as bride to the little pink king.

"Don't worry, my Prince," said the wolf. "Take the Princess into the forest. I know a bit of magic, and I can easily change my shape into that of your Princess, so that the King will think I am Helen. Leave the Princess in the forest and take me in my new shape to the King. Once he has given you the horse, take it, collect the Princess from the forest and ride like the wind. Only, before you have gone far, stop to think of me, for by doing that you will change me back to my own shape and I shall be able to run after you."

Helen ran off into the black forest, and the wolf gave one little shake of his tail. Immediately he became the mirror-image of the fair Princess. Ivan took the wolf-maiden by the hand and was delighted when King Afran immediately handed over the golden-maned horse in return for what he thought was going to be his beautiful bride. Ivan mounted the horse, refused to stay for supper, and rode off into the forest to find Helen. They were so glad to see each other that it was quite a minute before they could spare a thought for the wolf.

And so, just as King Afran was putting his fat pink fingers into those of his bride she turned into a great, grey, slavering wolf which snapped at his sixty-six swordsmen and padded off into the forest to join the young couple.

Now the Princess rode on the golden horse and Ivan rode on the wolf's back, and so they went on until they came to the bright brass gates of King Dolmat's palace.

"My friend," said Ivan, "I desperately need the firebird, but it seems a shame to hand over this beautiful horse to King Dolmat. What can we do?"

"Don't worry, my Prince," said the wolf. "Send Helen and the horse into the forest and leave the rest to me." So Ivan did as he was told, and then with a shake of his tail the wolf turned into a mirror-image of the horse with the golden mane. Ivan led this wolf-horse to King Dolmat who fairly scratched himself purple with pleasure and immediately handed over the firebird. As soon as Ivan was outside the gates the King prepared to mount his new horse for a ride; but as he lifted up his dirty foot into the stirrup he found himself getting instead on to the back of a great, grey, slavering wolf. This wolf snarled ferociously at the King and spat at the thirty-three spearsmen, and then was gone like the wind to join Ivan and Helen and the firebird.

Now everybody was happy, and as soon as the palace of the old Tsar came in sight the friendly grey wolf said goodbye to the young Prince and his bride, who thanked him profusely for his help. Then Ivan and Helen sat down under a tree at the edge of the forest, thinking that their troubles were over. But suddenly who should come out of the forest but Ivan's two elder brothers and they were more than a little upset to see Ivan with all that they had failed to find. Swearing a terrible oath Vasily drew his sword, and before Ivan had time to defend himself he dealt him such a dreadful blow that his head went spinning from his shoulders. Ivan was dead, and the two wicked brothers seized Helen and the horse and the firebird.

"Breathe but one word of what you have just seen," said Dimitry, "and I will personally chop you up into the finest mincemeat."

Great was the rejoicing at the court of the old Tsar when Dimitry and Vasily rode in bringing the Princess and the horse and the firebird. But Helen would do nothing but sit and weep at the thought of her dead Ivan, and nothing would make her smile or look happy.

The old Tsar, for his part, was absolutely overjoyed. He gave Dimitry half his kingdom immediately and arranged that Vasily should have the horse with the golden mane, and should marry Princess Helen as soon as possible. Preparations began for a really splendid royal wedding.

However, it so happened that the grey wolf was walking through the black trees when he spotted the head and body of his friend Ivan.

"What?" he said. "After all my trouble, here is my young friend without his head. Well I may be able to change my

shape but I cannot bring the dead back to life. Somehow I must get hold of a drop of the Water of Life and Death from the pool at the edge of the Earth."

Looking up he saw an old black crow and her son sitting in a tree.

"Old crow," he called, "you remember how I saved your son when he was a little one from being eaten by the black eagle? Now do me a favour in return."

"Aaaak," said the crow and fluttered her tattered wings.

"Please fly to the edge of the Earth for a drop of the Water of Life and Death from the pool there. Carry some back in your beak to sprinkle on the head and body of my poor young friend here. Hurry!"

"Aaaak," said the old crow again, and then she and her son flew like black arrows eastwards towards the edge of the Earth. Within hours they were back and miraculously, as they spattered the head and body with water from their beaks, the Prince came to life again and sat up rubbing his eyes.

He told the wolf what had happened, and the grey beast's jaws snapped in anger. "Get on my back," he snarled, and charged off vengefully towards the Tsar's palace where they were just in time to put a stop to all the marriage preparations.

As soon as the old Tsar heard Ivan's story, and saw the slavering jaws of the great grey wolf menacing the throats of Vasily and Dimitry, he proclaimed Ivan as his heir. Ivan straightaway married the fair Princess declaring that the wedding feast was far too splendid to waste. As for the two wicked brothers they were thrown down one hundred and thirty-two stone steps to a very damp and incredibly filthy dungeon where they spent the rest of their miserable lives.

Monster-Slayer

It was evening. Down at the water's edge small black waves slapped against the greasy stones. Low trees, bent by the cold winds which howled across the desolate plains, hung their night black shadows over the lake and tangled snake-like roots in the deep water. Some distance away from the bank, where the grey mist wreathed over the surface, there was a sudden boiling in the water and a shape surfaced and vanished again in a muddy wash. The few birds that were roosting nearby for the night, rose nervously and flew away from the lake. Nothing else moved. Life seemed to have stopped. And then on to the beach, out of the black water, crawled Grendel. He stood erect, shook the water from his shaggy body and, raising steel-sharp claws to the moon, howled like a wolf. His green eyes rolled and his scaly nose wrinkled as he snuffled in the wind; then he shambled off into the gathering darkness.

An hour or two away, near the sea-coast, the great Hall of Hrothgar, chief of the Danes, was ablaze with warmth and light. Packed into it were the strong thanes, sitting on the smooth benches and feasting the evening away. Roars of laughter mingled with the shouts of the warriors and every now and again a sweet stillness made welcome the reedy voice of Hrothgar's minstrel telling again in song the old tales of brave deeds, great men and rich rewards.

As the minstrel's thin voice died away the cries of appreciation rose. Hrothgar spoke in a voice still strong in spite of his years.

"Now, thanes of Denmark and great warriors. Night is falling and Heorot, our famous Hall, will soon be empty.

I need not tell you of the fate that threatens any who stay here when Grendel, stalking through the echoing night, comes searching for human food to satisfy his foul appetite."

Several of the men began to look around nervously and there was a clatter as one of them knocked an ale-horn on to the stone-paved floor.

"Are we so fearful that we shall run like mice? Is there not one of us who will wait and fight the monster?" asked Hrothgar.

Heads dropped and dark eyes flickered from side to side. No one, not even those who had drunk deeply from the mead-cup, would spend a night in Heorot. Too many good, fair men had paid with their lives since that first night when Grendel had murdered thirty of the strongest warriors in the Hall, laughing and screeching as their sharp swords bent on his shaggy hide, and spears rebounded harmlessly or snapped into splinters.

Nobody would stay there. One by one the warriors slunk away.

So it had gone on for years, and so might it have gone on for many more years after that except that one day there came to Heorot a group of visitors from over the sea. It happened like this.

Hrothgar and his thanes, together with Wealthow his Queen, were together at their food when the doors opened and the door-keeper appeared. Behind his broad-shoulders could be seen more men, armed and armoured, wearily standing and waiting for permission to enter the Hall. The door-keeper strode forward and spoke to his King.

"Lord," he said. "Here is Beowulf, a thane from the land of the Geats, together with many fair warriors. He claims to have lived here as a young boy, and he has come a long sea-road to speak to you about what he says are great matters."

Hrothgar rose from his bench and went to the doors himself to welcome the young Geat and his warriors. Beowulf was fair, taller by a head than anyone else in the Hall, and had eyes as blue and as cold as the deepest Northern fjord.

"My errand is simple, Lord Hrothgar," he said in a voice as bleak as his eyes. "I come to repay the debt I owe to you and your throne, a debt owed since you gave shelter to me and my father many years ago. If it had not been for your protection we should both have been slain by our enemies."

He knelt at Hrothgar's feet. "Now let me try to repay that debt by ridding Heorot of that nightly visitor whose evil deeds are spoken of in lands far and near."

"Gren ... del ..." murmured the gathered warriors, dropping out the syllables as though afraid to utter them.

"Grendel," said Beowulf firmly. "Give me leave, Hrothgar, to wait here tonight so that I can meet this Grendel!"

The lovely Queen, Wealthow, bent her head close to Hrothgar's ear so that her dark hair brushed his face. Hrothgar rubbed his chin and looked doubtful.

"No, Wealthow," he said at last. "It is my duty as King of this land to give this young man the chance he asks for, even if – as you suggest – he dies here forlorn and alone."

Wealthow withdrew again behind her husband's chair, but her eyes burned with pity for the fair young man from the land of the Geats. If only she could have had a son like this great warrior!

But then there was another voice heard, that of Unferth, a favourite of Hrothgar.

"Wait, King!" he said, his face flushing with shame, anger and jealousy as he caught the admiring glances falling Beowulf's way. "Before you give this – this Geat – the right to fight for the Danes, let me tell you what sort of man he is."

Beowulf moved slowly down the table and, shouldering his warriors aside, towered over the seated Unferth.

"Speak, then," he said. "What sort of man am I?"

Unferth stood up and spoke out. "I have heard that you are a boaster, a braggart, a man who once recklessly risked his own life and that of his friend by challenging him to see who could stay longest in the deep and icy sea."

The blue eyes darkened. "Go on."

"And I heard that after seven days and nights the other proved stronger than this braggart here, but that he struggled ashore and has ever since told how he stayed there longer."

"Is that all?"

"That is surely enough. Hrothgar will never, if he has sense, entrust such a struggle to a windbag, to an empty . . . an empty thing."

Beowulf turned his back on Unferth, put one sandalled foot on a stool and flung his arms wide as if in appeal.

"Boaster? Empty thing, am I? You, Unferth, because of your jealousy, speak in half-truths. True, a friend and I did swim by challenge in the sea, but not recklessly. We did it to prove to each other our great strength and that was what happened. Five nights we swam, Unferth, in the cold and black waves, and night after night I fought with naked sword against sharp-tusked sea monsters and scaly creatures of the deep. But I am the bravest of all warriors for after seven nights the sea cast me up on the shore, together with the bodies of nine monsters. Not even the raging sea dare hold me any longer!"

Unferth said nothing, but Beowulf drew his long sword and held it, hilt forward, towards him.

"Here," said the tall Geat. "Since I am only an empty boaster and you are so brave, take my sword. I will sleep in Hrothgar's Hall tonight while you stay in Heorot to fight Grendel. Agreed?"

Unferth made no answer, but turned away and, followed by all the other thanes, went out into the darkness.

Hrothgar and Wealthow went last of all, calling on the gods to look down kindly on Beowulf and his Geat warriors who were to face the menace of the terrible Grendel. One last warning was given by Hrothgar.

"Remember, Beowulf, no earthly weapon will harm Grendel, for he is covered with hair and scales so thick that no sword can cut him."

"Fear not!" answered Beowulf, and he stripped off his tunic to show Hrothgar knotted muscles and mighty sinews. "These are the weapons I shall use, for I mean to kill him with my bare hands. Now good-night, Hrothgar; tomorrow is another day."

Once the Danes had left, Beowulf and his men stretched their sea-weary legs out along the wooden benches. The talk dwindled into murmurs and as the candles guttered low Heorot fell into a deep silence. All slept save one. Beowulf waited.

From across the marshes came the mere-song of Grendel. He shambled up to the closed doors, grunted with anger when he found them barred, and then, lifting steel-clawed arms, he tore his way into the Hall. Cries of horror came from the Geats as the shaggy, green-eyed shape bulked in the doorway, followed by wild despairing screams as the monster fell on the nearest warrior and killed him with one blow.

But then Beowulf, with a shout of anger, leapt across the body of his friend and grabbed Grendel by the arm. He knew spears and swords would be of no use, and he put all his faith in the vast strength of his hands and wrists. With a twist and a heave he tried to throw the monster on to his back. Grendel stood firm, but for the first time in his long life he felt fear. He pulled away, anxious now only to escape, but Beowulf held firm. Muscles cracked as each pulled and heaved and struggled. Grendel aimed a scarring blow at Beowulf's face, then howled with pain as the Geat warrior with iron hands tugged and twisted the hairy arm.

Then Grendel knew that he had met a mightier strength than his own. His one thought now was to escape. He fought silently, straining, until with a wild yell he tore himself free and escaped into the darkness. With him went a dying wail

13

and a scream that made the strong men listening in Heorot clap their hands over their ears with horror. And there, inside Heorot, was Beowulf, astride the dead body of his friend but holding with fingers that had never slackened their grip, the wrist, arm and shaggy shoulder of the monster, torn from his body in the short struggle. Deep red blood had dripped from the severed arm on to the stone floor. Beowulf waved the arm high in the air in triumph and his men cheered.

Away in their own sleeping halls Hrothgar and his court heard the cheering and came running with torches, exclaiming at the sight of the monster Grendel's arm which the youngest Geat had by that time nailed to the highest beam of Heorot.

"Grendel is as good as dead," said Hrothgar, "since neither man nor fiend could live with a wound like that. Give the day over to rejoicing!"

Beowulf was put at the high table and for the rest of the night and all the next day a great feast went on. Gifts were showered on the warrior and everyone sang his praises; even the once-jealous Unferth begged Beowulf's forgiveness for his earlier foolishness.

So the next night Geats and Danes lay down side by side to sleep in the great Hall, thinking that at last they were safe. But they would not have slept at all had they known what fate was creeping across the marshes towards them.

For, unknown to them, Grendel had not lived alone in the black mere. His mother, equally fierce, also lived there. When she saw the body of her only son lying at the edge of the reeds, the spot where he had finally died, she set out at once to avenge his death.

Swiftly she sped across the misty marsh towards sleeping Heorot, making no noise at all. Then with a tremendous crash she burst open the great doors. All in one swift movement she killed one of the sleeping Danes, leapt into the air to tear Grendel's arm from the high beam, and disappeared again, howling into the darkness.

Beowulf who had been sleeping elsewhere was roused from his bed by loud cries of panic and, by torchlight, he and Hrothgar listened to the wild stories of those shivering thanes who had seen Grendel's mother. Then, tired as he was, he put on his steel corslet and helmet, and reached for his sword. But Unferth stepped forward holding out a bright blade.

"Here, Beowulf," he said, "take my sword. It is called Hrunting and has served many brave warriors through fearsome battles. If any edge can cut into the hide of Grendel's mother, then Hrunting can!"

Beowulf put one hand on Unferth's shoulder and thanked him; then without a word he turned and set off in search of the monster. The trail was easy to follow for the dying Grendel had left blood-stains by the beaten-down track. Before long the little band of silent men stood at the mere's edge, gazing down into the foul black water. Strange shapes, like those of sea monsters, moved and swirled in the depths, but the mighty Beowulf was not afraid.

"I who killed Grendel am not afraid of his mother," he said, and then with a strong leap, sword in hand, he plunged into the murky water and disappeared from view. The watchers saw the waves and the spray die away and then there was silence except for quiet ripples among the reeds at the mere's edge.

Beowulf had hardly entered the water before he was seized by the monster. The two wrestled as they sank, and only Beowulf's armour saved him from the fangs and claws of his enemy. Down and down they sank, lungs bursting for air, down and down and then reaching the ribbed sand at the bottom, rolled still fighting into the entrance to an underwater cave: Grendel's lair. Inside the cave they rose again until Beowulf's head broke surface so that he could suck in the air of the cave.

Grendel's mother attacked him again and again, and

although the Geat struck at her with the sword Hrunting he could not harm her. Even that remarkable weapon was useless against her, for she seemed to be ten times more powerful than her dead son.

As the monster searched for a weapon to finish the fight Beowulf saw the one last chance he needed. A huge sword hung on the cave wall, glowing with a magic fire. Shouting his war-cry he swung it in an arc through the air and chopped at the monster's neck. True as the flight of a swooping hawk it sang on its way and Grendel's mother gave one final scream before falling at Beowulf's feet, her grisly head almost parted from her shoulders. Panting, the Geat dragged himself along the cave floor to the edge of the water where he suddenly noticed the dead body of Grendel lying where his mother had placed him. Once more Beowulf raised that terrible sword and this time he sliced Grendel's head clean off so that the blood poured into the black waters of the mere.

Up above on the bank the watchers had long given up hope of ever seeing Beowulf again. Sadly they turned away from the dreaded lake, crying out in fear and anguish. Only Unferth remained. Suddenly they heard him call out in astonishment. Turning, they saw him pointing down into the mere.

"Look," he cried, "the black waters are turning red as if with blood! And now, look again, the red and black are clearing, and the lake is pure again. Look comrades, look there!"

Rising through the water, now clear and sparkling, swam Beowulf, dragging behind him the huge and gruesome head of Grendel.

It was a joyful little procession back to Heorot. Three men carried Grendel's head on the points of their spears, and loud and long were the rejoicings at their triumphant return. Costly presents were again heaped on Beowulf so that at last when he and his men set sail, their sea-goer rode lower in the waves for the weight of the gifts. Beowulf stood in the prow with his eyes never turning back, but Hrothgar and Wealthow watched from the edge of the cliffs until the oar-songs of the Geats faded in the crash of the surf and the striped war-sail dipped over the horizon.

Thor and Loki Visit the Giants

Of course after it was all over Loki refused to admit that he had been fooled. He declared that he had known all along that Thor was being tricked, but that he had kept quiet because there had always been the chance that Thor might prove triumphant. "Such mighty strength!" Loki would say with his black grin. "Such huge bands of muscles on the arms of the Hammer-Bearer. Oh, if only *all* the gods were as strong and as clever as Thor here, we should soon rid the place of those evil giants." And Thor would scowl and lower his bushy eyebrows, never sure whether Loki was poking fun at him or not.

The whole thing had begun one day when Loki, Thor and Thor's young servant, Thialfi, decided to pay a visit to the home of the giants. They had been boasting about their strength and cunning to the other gods, and as the tall cups of wine were drained their boasts grew fuller, until almost without realising what they were saying they found themselves accepting a challenge to make the visit. Having accepted the challenge, of course, Thor was too stubborn, Loki too cunning and Thialfi too frightened to go back on their words.

And so early next morning the three set out, their heads still light from the fumes of the previous night's wine. Each had a thonged leather pack on his back, and each faced the journey in a different way. Thor carried his famous hammer on his shoulder and tramped along solidly, face firmly set towards the giants' land far ahead. Thialfi skipped and sang lightly by his side, occasionally racing off like the wind and returning out of breath but revelling in his gift of speed over the ground. Loki alternately joked and grumbled, sometimes going on ahead and sometimes falling behind, but always keeping up an endless rattle of jokes, insults, wild exaggerations and boasts about what he was going to do to the first giant they met.

As evening drew near Thor announced that they should find a safe place to sleep for the night.

"Tired, are you?" sneered Loki. "Of course you little creatures soon need to rest. As for me I'm good for miles yet, but since you cannot carry your tiny hammer any farther I suppose we'd better do as you suggest. If Thialfi will stop behaving like a swallow with its tail on fire he might help us look for a good place to stay."

At the time they were passing through a big forest which looked far from safe so they pressed on to the far edge, and as they came out of the trees they saw in the gathering gloom a vast hall in front of them. The entrance to the hall seemed to be as wide as the building itself, but the inside seemed dry and empty, and there were several smaller rooms leading off the main one. There were no benches or stools in any room, so they chose one of the smaller chambers and settled down on the floor to sleep. Loki and Thialfi slept well, but Thor's sleep was disturbed by odd groans and rumbles from somewhere close by, so he spent most of the night on guard sitting in the doorway with his hammer across his knees and peering out into the black night.

Thor's suspicions proved well founded when the first rays of morning sunshine slotted through the leaves and fell on the mountainous form of a giant, lying on the ground nearby, fast asleep. Thialfi was all for running away before he woke up, but Thor was braver and Loki was always ready for a bit of devilment. Running up to the giant's head, he climbed into his ear and bellowed into it at the top of his voice. The giant yawned and slowly sat up, rubbing his eyes. Then, catching sight of Loki, he grinned, showing a fine row

of white teeth, each one as large as the great table in the gods' dining hall.

"Hail mighty gods. Hail Thor," grinned the monster, putting his vast, moon-like face close to the ground and squinting at the three tiny figures down below. "My name is Skrymir and I was out looking for you, my beauties."

The gods looked at each other in surprise, but Skrymir continued. "We heard that you were on the way so I was sent to bring you safely to our little halls. So come on, and I'll show you the way."

The gods were ready to go, and on Loki's suggestion they put all their own belongings into the giant's pack so that he could carry the lot for them. Then Skrymir began to look round as if he had lost something.

"Now where did I put my dratted glove?" rumbled the giant, and then grunted with satisfaction as he picked up the strange hall they had slept in. They had in fact spent the night in the thumb of the giant's right gauntlet!

The four spent the whole of that day travelling across wild and rough country, and then as night fell the giant lay down to sleep in an oak forest, telling the three friends to get their own supper out of his wallet where all the things were packed. Thor was hungry, but although he struggled with the knot in the thongs which bound the wallet, and even though he used all his tremendous strength, he failed to undo it. Loki didn't help matters by poking fun all the time at Thor's failure, and Thialfi did nothing but sit singing a sad little song about there being no supper. Eventually Thor completely lost his temper, picked up his hammer and dealt the sleeping giant a tremendous blow on top of his head with it, a blow that would have split a boulder into pieces, but Skrymir just shook his head a little, opened one eye wide and looked at them.

"A leaf must have fallen on me," he said. "Aren't you asleep yet, my beauties?" And he shut his eyes again.

23

Thor tried to sleep but hunger, anger and fear combined to keep him awake, and at last he sprang up, grabbed his hammer again and in sheer fury struck such a blow at the top of the giant's head that it made a dent in the round skull. But Skrymir just shook his head, opened one eye and looked sleepily at Thor.

"I think a little bird must have dropped a piece of moss on me," he said. "Are you still not asleep, my tiny friends?"

Thor trembled at the unbelievable strength of this mighty giant, but determined to have one more try to hurt him. Swinging his hammer round his head he charged across the grass, leapt into the air with both feet and brought it down like a thunderbolt on Skrymir's head; it was such a blow that the hammer sank into the bony skull right up to the handle before it came out again. At that the giant sat up and scratched his bristly head.

"Can't seem to get to sleep tonight," he grumbled. "Now an acorn's fallen on me. Ah well, it's as good as morning so perhaps we'd better be making a move." He pointed into the distance where the tops of vast halls could be seen rising out of the morning mists. "See," he said, "there is the giant's city of Utgard, and there you are sure to find a warm welcome. My task is done, so I must leave you." And gathering up the wallet he disappeared, leaving the gods still hungry but glad to see the back of him for all that. When he was a safe distance away Loki put his thumb to his nose and called after the broad back in the distance, "Coward! Just when I was going to punch your fat head too."

Thor and his companions passed under the mighty archway of the entrance to Utgard, marvelling at the towering buildings which stretched up into the clouds; wondering at the fountains as big as waterfalls and at the rows of stone statues, each one as tall as Skrymir. The gods gaped around in amazement but were soon spotted by another shambling giant who led them into a cavernous dining hall where ten or more were sitting at a table, eating, drinking and laughing. At their entrance all noise stopped and the chief giant welcomed them, lifting each one carefully on his horny hand to the surface of the table.

"Welcome, mighty Thor," said the Chief in a voice of thunder, and the table shook beneath their feet as the rest murmured a cheerful welcome. "We have heard of your great feats of strength," the Chief went on, "and we are happy to see you. My name is Loki-Utgard."

"Well, at least you've got half of a good name," said Loki, for once in his life feeling subdued and weak. The table shook again, and Loki-Utgard put his grizzly beard close to where Loki stood, feet apart and looking defiant. Each hair on the beard was like a wire rope.

"What can *you* do, tiny-toes?" murmured the giant in a whisper that lifted the black hair on Loki's head as if a great gale had blown through it. "Can you use the mighty Thor's hammer, or a similar weapon?"

"Such idle weapons are not for me," shouted Loki. "But I can eat. Yes, I *can* eat. I wager I can eat more and faster than anyone in the hall."

Again there was a rumble of the table, and then large hands were setting a trough made of thick wood on the floor. The trough seemed to be as long as ten men stretched head to toe, and it was full of steaming joints and hunks of meat. A most delicious smell filled the air, and Loki licked his lips as he remembered that he had had no food for a very long time. He was put at one end of the trough and one of the younger giants knelt at the other. Then as the Chief bellowed out the word to begin, they both began to eat their way towards the middle.

Loki packed in the meat till his hands dripped grease, his jaws ached from chewing and his stomach bulged under his black tunic. He ate well and quickly, but fast as he ate the giant at the other end was equally fast. At last the two met, and there was a roar of delight from all as they saw that the two had met in the very middle of the trough. And Loki would have claimed a victory, or at least a draw, except that while he had just eaten the joints of meat, his opponent had eaten the meat, the bones and the wooden trough as well, splinters, nails and all!

Loki went into a corner to sulk, and nothing was heard from him for quite a time except for great grunts of indigestion.

Thialfi had quite enjoyed watching Loki being beaten, and he was sure that he could do a lot better, so he offered to race on foot against any giant who dared take up his challenge, stating with confidence that he could outrun anyone over any distance. So the whole company trooped outside. The Chief scrawled a line in the dust with his club and pointed to a tall spruce tree in the distance. "Round that tree, then," he said, "and the first one back here shall be the winner." Thialfi tightened his belt and toed the scratch line while a lumbering giant named Hugi came forward to run against him.

As the Chief called "Go!" Thialfi was off like the wind, but Hugi ran so quickly that his movement was a blur against the sky. The spruce leaned over at the wind made by his turning and he was back at the starting line before Thialfi had gone more than twenty paces.

Thialfi was down-hearted but not finished. "Shall we make it the best of three?" he suggested, and so it was agreed. The second race, however, proved little different from the first. Thialfi had barely gone thirty paces before Hugi was passing him on the way back!

"Once more," he said, and this time the very grass turned brown with the speed of Thialfi's running. But still he had only gone about forty paces before Hugi was being cheered in at the finishing line.

Thialfi went to join Loki in his corner, and it was left to Thor to uphold the honour of the gods. "How shall we

try your strength, O mighty Hammer-Bearer?" asked Loki-Utgard. A snort from the corner might have been Loki grunting sarcastically, or it might just have been a final grumble of indigestion. It certainly wasn't Thialfi who was stretched out like a long green leaf, wilted after the three races and still trying to get his breath back again.

Thor drew his fair eyebrows down over blue eyes. "Anything!" he said quietly and tightened his grip on the great hammer.

"Drinking, then?" said the giant. Thor nodded. It was not quite what he had expected, but he was sure that no one could surpass him at that game. He waited and soon a large drinking-horn was presented to him full of a deep red wine. Thor wiped his mouth and took a pull at the horn that would have emptied an ordinary drinking cup. No result. Thor looked at the wine, slackened his belt, put both arms round the horn and drank again. But as he put the horn down it was plain to see that hardly any of the wine had gone at all.

"Last go," said Loki-Utgard. "Come on, Thor, even our weakest giant can finish this tiny cup in three draughts. Drink, man, drink, don't sip."

Thor blew out his breath, wiped his beard and this time drank until his ear-drums cracked and the sweat started from his broad forehead. But deep as he drank – and no god could have drunk deeper than Thor that day – it had little effect on the horn-cup for when he finished it seemed very little emptier than when he had started.

A roar of applause from the watching giants startled Thor, and he at once thought that they were mocking him. Turning furiously to Loki-Utgard he threw out the next challenge – "Weight-lifting!"

Loki-Utgard smiled a little. "Why, little one," he said, "I doubt if you could even lift my poor cat." And he pointed to a grey mouser standing in the doorway. Thor strode over, hiccuping a little from the wine, and put his shoulder under the cat's furry stomach. But heave as he might, and strain as he would, he could not lift the cat. The best he could do was to get one paw just off the ground.

Again the giants roared applause, and again Thor thought they were making fun of him. Furious now he stripped off his tunic and turning to face the giants challenged anyone to wrestle with him. There was a short silence, then the Chief said, "O mighty Thor, we would not like to hurt you. Wrestle if you must, but let it be with our old grandmother there. She has no teeth and is around seven hundred years old, but she is fond of a little wrestling still when the mood takes her."

Thor, infuriated, threw himself at the old woman, but she stood as firm as a rock, bending little, and gradually, as Thor's strength faded, she forced the god on to one knee.

"Enough!" called Loki-Utgard. "Our guests have proved their strength – or lack of it. No more for now. Let us cement our friendship with food, wine, song and laughter." And the three gods were carried back to the table where the rest of the evening was spent merrily enough, though sleep came none too soon for the exhausted friends.

The next morning proved to be a sunny one, and Thor, Loki and Thialfi were light-hearted as they made their farewells and thought of going home. They all said to the giants how foolish they must have seemed in trying to pit their tiny strength against that of their hosts. Then they set their faces towards the gate and were about to go, when they were stopped by Loki-Utgard.

"Wait!" he called. "I just cannot let you go thinking that you were weaklings yesterday. Let me tell you how you have been tricked ever since you came into our land." He paused and then went on. "Even in the forest before you reached here you were being fooled. That wallet of food that Skrymir invited you to open was tied up with

29

iron cable. No wonder you could not undo the knot with your bare hands! And, Thor, when you thought you were hitting Skrymir on the head with your hammer you were deceived. You were really hitting the side of the mountain, and if you look on your way back you will see three new deep valleys made from the dents caused by your blows that night."

The listening group of giants clapped. Loki-Utgard then turned to Loki.

"And you, my black-headed friend, are truly a mighty eater. But even you could not eat against our champion, because although you thought you were competing against a giant, in fact you were really competing against nothing else but Fire which had no difficulty in eating meat, bones and trough. But in spite of that you did very well."

The listening group of giants clapped again.

Loki-Utgard now spoke to Thialfi. "You can indeed run very fast, faster than any one of us, but our champion was no giant. It was Thought, and Thought runs quicker than the fastest god or the fastest giant ever could. But in spite of that you did very well."

The listening group of giants raised a cheer.

Loki-Utgard at last turned again to Thor. "What strength!" he roared, and the listening group of giants sighed a long, deep sigh. "Here is someone who drinks deeply, not knowing that the cup he was trying to drain was really connected to the Great Sea. Watch as you go home and notice how your efforts made the tide run back down the long beach."

Again a sigh from the giants.

"But what about the cat? That little grey animal was not a cat. It was really just one part of the great Midgard Serpent which encircles the Earth. You lifted it so much that you almost pulled its tail out of its mouth, and if that had happened who knows what might have been the result?"

A huge sigh from the giants.

30

"Finally, your wrestling. My friend, you were deceived into thinking that you were wrestling with an old woman but you were not. You were wrestling with Old Age itself, and as you know, Old Age eventually lays the strongest person helpless in the dust."

Thor, Loki and Thialfi had stood listening in silence and amazement, their pride swelling inside them as Loki-Utgard unfolded his tale. Then came cheer after cheer from the giants as the three gods, their steps springy now, strode out underneath the great archway and left Utgard for ever.

And as they emerged into the sunlight on the other side, Loki began to say, "Of course, I was not fooled for a minute! I knew all along.... Here, wait for me!"

The Story of Daedalus and Icarus

A spoilt boy needs a strong father. That is undoubtedly true. But then a boy with a strong father would naturally not be spoilt. Thus mused Daedalus, the King's architect, as he wandered along the summer sea-shore, listening to the gulls' squawking and quarrelling, and watching their endless swooping and wheeling and diving. He kicked with his sandal at a pebble and sent it skittering through the dry sand, amused at his own thoughts. Tonight he would tell them to King Minos, making a riddle of them: "What is it that a spoilt boy needs but can never have?" It should amuse the King and perhaps he would give Daedalus more gold for the work he had done recently. The architect smiled again at the thought but then looked upwards sharply as a cry came from above.

"Father!" the word fell on the wind from the cliff-top. High above him Daedalus could see his son Icarus, standing on the very edge of the cliff where the rocks were crumbling, his arms spread as if he were about to dive on to the rocks below.

"No!" cried Daedalus, his heart in his mouth. "No, Icarus! Go back!"

With a mocking laugh the boy dropped his arms and stepped back from the edge of the cliff. It had been just another of his stupid tricks.

As Daedalus walked on along the beach he worried about his son, knowing that if he had been a strong father Icarus would have been beaten many times for trying to scare him and worry him, for no reason other than devilment. But then – he shrugged and his lips twisted wryly as he remembered the saying "Strong men don't have spoilt sons".

32

Another shout made him turn to see two of King Minos' men running down the beach towards him.

"Daedalus!" they shouted. "King Minos needs you immediately."

The architect was surprised but rather pleased. Perhaps Minos was going to offer him the new building job for which he had hoped. He turned and walked quickly back to the Palace, laughing and chattering with the soldiers. He waited in the cool marble hall while a message was taken in to Minos to say that he had arrived.

Daedalus looked around the familiar hall which he himself had designed and built as an addition to the Palace several years ago. He admired the painted frescoes on the walls showing Cretan youths and maidens running, hurling spears and leaping over slab-bodied bulls. He thought about having similar frescoes painted on the walls of the Labyrinth – that underground maze of black tunnels he had built for Minos. But no, it was so dark in the maze that no one would see them – and in any case no one lived long enough to appreciate paintings there. The Minotaur was swift and merciless in his killing.

The architect's thoughts were suddenly interrupted by a bellow of rage from within. He took quick steps into the King's room, where he found Minos, legs astride and arms raised above his head, absolutely furious. The two soldiers were cowering before him, one holding the left side of his face which showed the fiery red imprint of the King's fingers. Minos turned and bore down on Daedalus like an enraged bull. Daedalus fell to his knees, afraid for his life, wondering what had happened to make the King so angry. He covered his face with his hands as he saw Minos reach towards the jewelled dagger at his belt.

"Stupid, blundering, incompetent idiot!" yelled the King. Daedalus flinched. He said nothing for there was nothing to say.

"Snivelling, lame-brained fool," said the King. "Get ready to die."

"But Lord, what have I done?" whimpered Daedalus.

The King drew back his sandalled foot and lashed out wickedly, but Daedalus threw himself backwards out of range across the floor.

"Daedalus," said the King in a quiet voice that was even more menacing than his bellow.

"Yes, my Lord King?"

"Do you remember the Labyrinth?"

"My Lord?"

How could he forget? It had been the biggest triumph of his life, building the maze so cleverly that nobody who set foot in it could ever again find his way out.

"No one can ever escape from it, so you said," Minos went on.

"That's right, my Lord, I'd stake my life on it."

"Then prepare to die. For last night, I'm told, your famous Labyrinth's secret was broken, my sacred Minotaur killed, and my most precious prisoner allowed to escape."

"But nobody could escape without help, my Lord."

The King roared again. "He *had* help, fool! Of course he had help. But in the end he escaped, and you had said he couldn't. And for that you will surely die." His hand again went towards the dagger, but then stopped.

"Take him away," he snarled at the soldiers. "Shut him in the tower while I make up my mind how to kill him slowly. One day and one night, Daedalus and then. . . ." He drew his finger across his fat throat with a hiss and then turned away.

Alone in the damp cell in the tower, Daedalus waited. Within the hour the door opened and his son Icarus was flung in beside him, crying, bewildered, all the tricks knocked out of him, but full of petulant questions.

Daedalus, for the first time in his life, spoke sharply, telling him to save his tears for when he had to die. The boy

34

went off to sulk in the corner while Daedalus paced the cell, thinking.

An hour went by and Icarus spoke. "Father," he said in his spoilt, whining voice, "you've got to get us out of here."

Daedalus ignored him, but then sighed, shrugged his shoulders and went over to the door to whisper through the keyhole.

"Pssst!" he hissed. Outside the guard shuffled his feet.

"Pssst! Guard!"

"What do you want, Daedalus?" The guard was one of the two who had brought him from the Palace, and an old friend.

"Do you like gold?"

"Do donkeys like strawberries?"

"Here then. I shall have no use for it soon." There was a tinkle as Daedalus pushed a coin through a crack between the timbers of the door.

"Would you like some more?"

"Yes, oh yes, Master Daedalus." The soldier sounded eager.

"Then open the door and I will show you gold, more gold than you have ever imagined."

The bolt creaked and the door opened. As the guard thrust his grizzled head into the cell, Daedalus with a sigh brought down a heavy stool on it. The guard collapsed in a heap and Daedalus and Icarus slipped down the stone steps and ran low towards the sea-cliffs as fast as their legs would carry them.

"Poor friend," thought Daedalus as they ran, thinking of the soldier. "Well, he didn't see gold but at least he saw golden stars!" He caught hold of his son's hand to help him over the rough tussocks of grass. Then he turned off the path, pushed aside the low branches of a flowering bush and scrambled through the entrance of a cave, dragging Icarus behind him. Inside it felt damp and there was little light, but at least they were safe for the time being, safe while Daedalus thought of a way to escape from the island.

Icarus was bad-tempered, full of nagging questions. "I don't like this cave, Father. Why can't we go back to our own home? Why is the King angry with us?"

"Quiet, Icarus, while I think."

The boy went sulkily towards the entrance of the cave where it was lighter and passed the time playing with some birds' feathers which he found on the floor. He lifted them above his head and let them drift down to the floor again. Daedalus watched, an idea slowly forming in his mind. If he could find enough feathers, and find something to hold them together, then he was sure he could make wings. With wings he and Icarus could leave the island safely and fly over the sea, out of the reach of King Minos.

"We'll fly!" he said loudly and stood up suddenly. "Now Icarus, for once listen carefully and do as you are told, for our lives depend on it. Run down to the beach and gather as many large gulls' feathers as you can find. Bring them back here. Don't argue, go at once."

"But Father," began the boy, then let out a sudden howl. For the first time in his life he felt the smack of his father's hand on the back of his head. The blow was painful but it served its purpose. Sobbing with rage and wounded pride Icarus scuttled off to do as he was told, while Daedalus walked to a nearby wood looking up into the trees.

Much later, as the sun was setting, Icarus and Daedalus returned to the cave. To give him credit, the boy had done well and had managed to gather a large pile of white and grey feathers. Daedalus too had found what he had looked for.

"See," he said, holding out his arms which were covered with red blotches.

"What happened, Father? Your arms look as if they've been stung by bees."

"And quite right too. You see I need something to keep

the feathers together when I make the wings, and I thought of wax. There's always wax in a bees' nest, but the bees don't usually like it when you take it off them." Daedalus smiled grimly.

It was a long night. Icarus slept fitfully on the damp sand, but Daedalus sat and worked at the mouth of the cave where the moonlight filtered through the flowery bush.

And when the sun's first rays came over the eastern horizon, the wings were ready. Icarus was very excited and fussed around while his father tore his tunic into lengths to fasten the wings to their shoulders. As soon as they were ready, the two moved out of the cave, looked around cautiously to make sure that they were not being followed and then went up to the highest point on the cliff.

Down below the surf foamed over the black rocks. Grey gulls launched themselves from tiny ledges and lay on the wind effortlessly. The cliff-top breeze ruffled the feathers on Daedalus' wings and once again Icarus was whining.

"Father, these wings are uncomfortable."

"Then the sooner we get them off the better. Now listen. When we are flying flap the wings strongly but slowly. That way you will be able to keep going for a long time. Fly low with me over the sea, so that if anything goes wrong we are not so high that a fall will hurt us. Are you ready?"

"Yes, Father, but . . ." The rest of the words were lost in a shrill scream as Daedalus lifted his hand, placed it in the small of his son's back and pushed him off the cliff's edge. The boy fell, wings flapping wildly, until at last, clumsily but then with more skill, he was flying! Daedalus held his breath, closed his eyes and then he too jumped to join Icarus in the air.

For a while the two spent time getting used to the wings and the strange wonderful new experience, but then Daedalus pointed out to sea and they headed away from the rising sun and away to freedom.

For a time all went very well. The wings were big and strong, and the two flew over the wave crests, feeling the spray cold on their trailing toes, laughing at the ease with which they were travelling. Daedalus felt hope rising inside him, and even began to think about their future when they finally reached the other side of the sea. Perhaps Sicily would be the best place for them to seek refuge, safe enough and far enough away from Minos to be out of reach and out of danger.

A delighted shout roused him from these thoughts and he looked up to see that his son had disobeyed his orders and was flying far above him, shouting to his father to admire his cleverness. As he watched Icarus spiralled again upwards.

"Come down!" called Daedalus, but his words, and the boy's reply were lost in the rush of the wind and the spray.

"Come down, you stupid boy!" called Daedalus, sobbing with dismay and anger. A new thought suddenly struck him. Apart from the danger of the boy falling to his death from such a great height, there was also another danger. Up there the sun would be hotter and would burn down on the wax – everyone knows wax melts in heat – and the wing feathers were only held together with wax . . .

"Come down, Icarus!" called Daedalus again. He started to go up himself after his son, but even as he rose he knew it was too late. There was a long frightened scream from above, a large struggling shape flashed past him, then came a faint splash from below. The cry hung on the wind for a second then it too was lost.

The sky was empty except for Daedalus, hovering and looking down. But the surface of the sea showed no trace of the few ripples that had been made when Icarus plunged downwards to his death.

Daedalus took a huge breath, then flew onwards towards Sicily. Inside his body he wept for the death of his son. The boy had always been spoilt, and if only he had been a stronger father then perhaps he would have been alive still. A solitary tear welled up in his eye and fell to the waves below. A gull squawked. And Daedalus flew on.

The Treasure of Rhampsinitus

Ahmed the builder was dying. He lay stretched out on his wooden bed while his two sons leaned over the curved rail at the foot of it and listened to his last words. Ahmed's wife held a silver drinking vessel to the old man's lips and helplessly watched his old fingers scrabbling over the richly embroidered bed-cloth.

Ahmed spoke, and the voice came out gratingly as if unwilling to leave the feeble body: "Setna, Kaptah, my sons. Come nearer."

The two young men bent forward to catch the words.

"You know what I am, my sons?"

"Yes Father," said the elder son, Setna. "You are a fine builder, the like of whose workmanship, in dressed stone and marble, will never be seen in this land again."

A thin dribble of moisture escaped from the corner of the old man's mouth. "Yes, a humble builder, my sons, that's what I was, but I was always able to live in a fine style, surrounded by rich objects. Did you never wonder where my money came from?"

"Father," said Kaptah, the younger son, "we know that you got it from King Rhampsinitus as payment for building the new treasure room at the royal palace."

A ghost of a smile visited Ahmed's face and his eyes opened wider for a second. "King Rhampsinitus gave me little enough for all my hard work. But listen, I am going to tell you a secret that could make your fortunes but could cost your lives. Listen."

The two young men waited.

"When I built the King's new treasure house," said

Ahmed, "I used the outer wall of the palace as one of the walls of the treasure chamber. This saved time and money. As you know, the King insisted that I should do all the building on my own, because he was afraid of too many people knowing where he kept his treasure. Working alone like that gave me the chance to loosen one of the slabs in the outer wall, to install a pivoting mechanism and to replace it so cunningly that no one could tell by looking at it that it had ever been moved."

The young men gasped. Now they began to realise where the money had really come from for all the fine things in their father's house. Now they could see why they had never been short of a sheep to sacrifice on feast days, or a skin of wine if friends arrived. Their father had been helping himself to the King's treasure through his own private entrance!

The old man was near death, but he talked on. "Listen, my sons. I have taken very little really. Just a coin or two at a time from the biggest jars and chests where no one could see the difference. I urge you to do the same, for I warn you, if you take too much at once the King will notice and your lives will be lost."

"Yes, Father," said Setna impatiently, "but you have not told us where to find the sliding block."

"On the west wall. Below the tallest watch-tower. Three courses of stones from the bottom. The square block with a picture of the god Osiris carved into it. Just push and it will open."

Shortly afterwards old Ahmed died and, leaving their mother to weep, the two sons slipped out of their house, through the narrow streets of the town and over the cool night sand to the walls of the King's palace. The moon shed a pale light on to the steep cliff of the west wall, and above them the young men could hear a guard coughing in the watch-tower. There was a rattle of dice from up there followed by a curse and a laugh.

Setna ran his fingers along the third course of bricks. Each block had a picture of one of the Nile gods on it, and the one with Osiris' head on it looked no different from the others. But when they pushed at it the clever pivoting arrangement came into operation. The stone slid to one side and Setna and Kaptah squeezed through the gap to find themselves standing inside Rhampsinitus' treasure house! A small oil-lamp burning in a niche on one wall threw flickering golden light on piles of strong chests, tall stone jars full to the top with coins, great ingots of gold and silver, and tumbled heaps of elephants' tusks. A sharp tang of spice was in the air and there, arranged against the far wall, were the ceremonial head-dress and golden ornaments worn by the King on royal occasions.

After getting over the shock of seeing so much treasure, Setna and Kaptah very quietly removed just a few coins from each of several jars and then, afraid of the silence and splendour, they left, closing the stone exit behind them.

But this was the first of many visits, and on each visit the two brothers began to get more and more greedy and careless. Eventually they reached the stage where they were filling sacks with coins, easing gold bars through the hole in the wall, and once even debating in whispers whether it would be safe to take King Rhampsinitus' second-best crown.

This greed was bound to lead to their downfall, for the treasury officials began to notice strange and unaccountable losses. Guards were doubled, and the doors sealed carefully, but each morning there would be a fresh mystery. So further steps were taken, and the next night as Setna tiptoed across the floor of the treasure chamber there was a loud crash and his leg was pinned by a monstrous-jawed iron mantrap. Escape was impossible for him, for the sharpened and probably poisoned teeth of the trap were already biting fatally into the flesh, and from outside the doors Kaptah could hear

the hubbub of guards alerted by the closing of the trap. What was to be done? His trapped brother would be recognised, even if he were dead, and within hours the whole family would be arrested and put to death.

Setna read the fear in his brother's eyes. "I am a dead man, Brother," he said, "so cut off my head at once, take it with you and make your escape. Be quick. Without my head the guards will never recognise me, and so you and the rest of the family will be safe."

The chains at the door were rattling, so Kaptah, wasting no more time, took the King's ceremonial sword off the wall, sliced his dying brother's head from his body and with that in the sack, and the sack in his hand, he made good his escape. The stone pivoted back into place just as the guards burst through the door to stand marvelling at the headless corpse in their trap.

King Rhampsinitus was enraged. "This was a clever thief," he said looking at Setna's body, "but an even cleverer one has escaped. Take this thing . . ." kicking at the corpse with his jewelled foot, "and hang it in chains in the bazaar. Guard it by day and by night, and tell the guards to watch out for any woman weeping nearby. Anyone found doing so should be brought straight to me, for she will be a relation of the thief."

Now Kaptah's mother was extremely upset at the sight of her elder son's body hanging in chains in the market-place, but she had too much sense to go very close. However, as the days went by she became so upset that she threatened to go and tell the King everything if Kaptah did not find some means of getting the body back to the house for proper burial.

And so on the next hot afternoon the two guards watching the body were amused at the antics of a young wine merchant driving three donkeys. Each donkey had four skins of fine wine, but somehow one skin on each donkey had come unfastened at the same time, so that wine began to flow in

46

three fine streams on to the sand in three different places. The young man seemed bewildered and didn't know which skin to try and stop leaking first, so he dashed from one donkey to another while the guards fetched cups and helped themselves to the rich red wine. And then, being rather kind, they helped the young man fasten up his skins again.

The merchant thanked them profusely for their help and offered them still more wine as a reward. Before very long the guards and the merchant were drinking far more than was good for them. The hot sun and the wine fumes soon took effect, and while the body swung in chains above, the guards fell into a fuddled slumber below.

As the snores began to rumble the young merchant got to his feet, unhooked his brother's body – for he was indeed Kaptah – loaded it on to one of the donkeys, covered it with a blanket, and ambled off to be quickly lost to sight in the narrow streets round the market-place.

This time King Rhampsinitus was almost apoplectic in his fury. "Can no one catch this clever thief?" he yelled. An answer came from a very unexpected quarter. His own daughter, the beautiful Nefer, suggested a plan, and this was it: the King was to send out heralds into all the market-places in the land, crying out that the King would give great riches and the hand of his favourite daughter, Nefer, to the man who could tell the best story of the cleverest and the wickedest thing he had ever done. If the thief came to tell his story to the Princess, for she was to hear all the stories, then she was to catch hold of him and hang on until the guards came to arrest him. And that would put an end once and for all to the thief.

Kaptah heard of the King's offer, and did not at all mind the idea of marrying the beautiful Nefer, so he quietly took his place in the line of men waiting to tell stories. At last his turn came and he strode into the darkened room where the Princess was sitting.

"Yes?" she said, attracted by the smiling eyes of the dark young man before her. "Go on then, bore me to tears with your story." She was getting rather tired as she had already heard forty-three tales that day.

"Well," said Kaptah, wasting no time, "the wickedest thing I ever did was cutting off my brother's head when we were robbing your father. And the cleverest thing was making the soldiers drunk so that I could steal his body to bury it."

"Guards!" screamed out the Princess, seizing hold of the young man's arm. But to her amazement what had appeared to be his arm came away in her hand, and when the guards arrived all they found was the Princess alone and gaping at an imitation arm made of leather stuffed with sand.

The King, when he heard of the clever thief's fresh success, was astonished by the man's wisdom, invention and boldness. Such a man ought to work for him, not against him, and so he again sent out messengers this time offering a free pardon to the thief and a rich reward.

Kaptah did not hesitate. He knew that the King was a man of his word so he walked boldly through the palace gateway and presented himself. King Rhampsinitus was impressed by his appearance, amazed at the story of how his treasure house had been robbed for years, and determined to give this man high honour. Nefer also liked the look of Kaptah now that she saw him again, and it was not long before the thief was not only the King's chief adviser but also his son-in-law. King Rhampsinitus never regretted his decision.

"The Egyptians are the most cunning people in the world," he often said, "but this man was the most cunning of all the Egyptians."

Now Who's Dead?

A fly, drawn by the sweet smell of honey, flew in through the onion-shaped window of the house of Abu Hassan in one of the poorer districts of Baghdad. It hovered over the centre of a rickety little table in the middle of which was one small cake on a cracked plate. On one side of the table sat Abu Hassan and on the other sat his beautiful young wife, Nouz-Hatoul. They sat silently watching the fly, waiting to see where it would settle.

"It's coming down on my side," whispered Nouz-Hatoul, her little pink tongue sliding over red lips.

"My side, I think, my love," said Abu, straightening his turban confidently.

The couple watched breathlessly until at last the fly stopped humming and landed right in the middle of the cake, where it sat smoothing its feelers with its front legs and preparing to probe the sugar icing of the cake with its long sticky tongue.

But it was not to have its feast after all. With a sigh Abu brushed it away, drew a short curved knife from his belt and sliced the cake accurately into two halves, giving one piece to his wife and cramming the whole of the other half into his wide mouth. He chewed, swallowed, and wiped the back of his hand over his mouth, watching Nouz-Hatoul delicately nibbling her share of the tiny sweetmeat. He dabbed at a crumb with a long forefinger and transferred it to his mouth.

"And so . . ." he said.

"The last food in the house," said Nouz-Hatoul.

"If the fly had landed on my side I should have won the bet and the cake would have been mine. But I should have given it all to you, my love."

"And if the fly had landed on my side I should have won the bet, and I might have given half to you," laughed Nouz-Hatoul.

The young couple looked seriously at each other.

"It really is the last food in the house," said Abu. "Since we have no more and there is nothing else left to sell, how are we to eat? How are we to live?"

Nouz-Hatoul frowned and said, "Before we were married you were the favourite courtier of our beloved Caliph. Nothing was too good for you."

Abu nodded. "And you were the favourite dancing-girl of the Caliph's wife, the beautiful Princess Bulbadur. Every day she used to load you with presents."

"And when we got married we got loads more presents . . ."

"And then we were told that we would have to leave the Palace, give up our jobs and go away to live happily ever after!"

They both sighed. The loss of their jobs had meant that they had no more money and no talents to get other jobs except dancing and being amusing. If only the Caliph and the Princess would give them back their old jobs at the Palace! But they knew that could never be for no married men and women ever worked there.

Abu again swatted at the fly. "Go away fly, there's nothing here for you. We might as well be dead." A sudden thought struck him. "Hey wait a minute, that's not a bad idea."

"What, to die?"

"No, of course not. But listen, my love. Supposing I were dead how would you find the money to bury me with?"

Nouz-Hatoul wrinkled her pretty little nose. "Well, I suppose I should have to go and beg the Princess to give me enough cloth to bury your body in and a few pieces of silver to pay for the funeral. But you're not dead, my dear husband."

"Oh, yes I am," said Abu and he leapt on the table, lay down flat on his back, crossed his arms over his chest and closed his eyes. "Dead as a doornail, my pet. Now pull the table-cloth over me and go and see what you can get out of the Princess!"

Nouz-Hatoul's eyes widened. "She will find out and have me flogged."

"She will never find out. Nobody from the Palace ever comes this far into the city. Now, be quick and do as I say."

Nouz-Hatoul knew how to act. She covered Abu with the table-cloth, went into the street and threw dust over her head, and then set out for the Palace weeping and wailing at the top of her voice, telling the world in no uncertain terms that her husband, the handsome Abu Hassan, was dead.

By the time she got to the Palace she had attracted a little crowd of curious urchins who followed her to the great gates and waited while she rang the bell. The guard who came in answer recognised her immediately and quickly showed her into the cool garden room where the Princess Bulbadur was sitting with her attendants. On hearing Nouz-Hatoul's story, the Princess clapped her hands softly and ordered that the poor widow should be given a large piece of the finest silk to bury her husband in, and a hundred pieces of silver as well. Nouz-Hatoul backed out of the room with her gifts, sobbing out her grateful thanks, but as soon as she was out of sight of the Palace she skipped home cheerfully and she and Abu did a little dance of joy.

But Abu had not finished yet. That was only the first part of his plan.

"Now my darling wife," he said, "it is your turn to die, and please do so quickly." So saying he pushed her on to the table, covered her with the table-cloth and staggered off, sobbing, towards the Palace.

52

Abu too knew how to act. He tore his clothes, uttered loud and anguished cries and broadcast the news of the death of his wife in such a voice that the Caliph had heard the noise long before his favourite was brought into the throne room.

"My dear boy," said the Caliph soothingly. "Don't distress yourself. I will see that she has a proper funeral, for I will give you a piece of the finest silk to bury her lovely body in, and a hundred pieces of silver as well."

Abu groaned his thanks, hid his tear-stained face and threw himself on to the ground to kiss the Caliph's feet.

But once in the street with his gifts he sped home and again he and Nouz-Hatoul did a little dance of joy round the old table. After which they made their way to the bazaar to buy food and drink and new clothes.

Back at the Palace the Caliph was still upset at the thought of the death of the beautiful Nouz-Hatoul. He knew how much his wife had loved the dark-haired dancing-girl, so he decided to visit the Princess in the garden room to give her words of comfort. But how astonished he was to find when he got there that she was just getting ready to go out, and apparently feeling quite cheerful.

"Have you not heard the bad news, then?" asked the Caliph.

"News?"

"Yes, the news that the beautiful Nouz-Hatoul is dead!"

"Rubbish," said the Princess. "Who told you that ridiculous story?"

The Caliph's grey beard bristled. He was not used to being told that he was talking rubbish. He spoke sharply: "Barely an hour ago I was visited by Abu Hassan who told me of the sad death of his wife. I thought the whole Palace would have heard by now. I gave him a piece of the finest silk and a hundred pieces of silver also, for I knew how much you loved her."

The Princess let out a shriek of laughter and collapsed on to one of the huge cushions that littered the marble floor. "And now I know that you're talking rubbish, for barely two hours ago I was paid a visit by Nouz-Hatoul herself who told me of the sad and sudden death of Abu. You've got it the wrong way round, you idiot!"

The Caliph's eyes sparkled with rage. "You're the idiot! *You've* got it the wrong way round, you little tadpole. I say that it is Nouz-Hatoul who is dead!"

"Abu Hassan is dead," said the Princess, in a calm voice now.

"Nouz-Hatoul!"

"Abu Hassan."

The Caliph looked as if he were about to burst a blood vessel. He pulled off his jewelled turban, threw it on the floor and stamped on it, while the Princess turned her back and, selecting a sugared date from a golden dish, sucked at it, saying no more.

At last the Caliph calmed down sufficiently to come up with an idea. Calling a guard he told him to run down to Abu's house and find out who really was dead. But Abu had suspected that this might happen, so when the guard peered through the window he could see Abu kneeling by the body of his wife and weeping. Triumphantly the guard turned and carried the news back to his master.

"Rubbish," said the Princess when she had listened to what he had to say. "The fool is lying to please you. I will send one of my girls to see."

But Abu had suspected that this also might happen and when the lady looked through the window she could see Nouz-Hatoul weeping over the body of her husband. She carried the news back triumphantly to her mistress.

"Rubbish," said the Caliph. "The fool is lying to please you."

They stood and thought and then the same idea came to both of them. "We will go ourselves to see who is dead!"

The coming of the Caliph and the Princess to the poor quarter of Baghdad caused a remarkable commotion. Market stalls were overturned as the people rushed to see the royal couple; children screamed and cheered as their fathers held them up high to see over the heads of the crowd; cats arched their backs and spat; dogs barked; and all the pigeons in the city rose high in the air at the sound of the royal trumpets and clapped their wings over Abu's house.

When the royal procession arrived at the little house, the Grand Vizier raised his jewelled staff and thumped with it on the door three times. Once! No answer. Twice! No answer yet. Three times! Still no answer.

"Go in," shouted the angry Caliph. Two guards opened the door to reveal a bare room, in the middle of which was an old table. On the table, surrounded by the remains of a rather grand feast, lay the dead bodies of Abu Hassan and Nouz-Hatoul, each covered with a piece of the finest silk and with tiny smiles on their faces. As people pushed in to see, the room got fuller and fuller of silent and puzzled watchers.

"Both dead?" said the Caliph, bewildered.

"Both? Dead?" said the Princess, equally bewildered, but thinking fast.

"Then Nouz-Hatoul died first," said the Caliph quickly.

"Not so, my dear husband, Abu died first."

"Is there never to be an end to this argument?" roared the Caliph, furious again, the points of his beard bristling. "I will give ten thousand pieces of silver to whoever can tell me which of these two poor people died first!"

Quick as a flash Abu was off the table and kneeling at the Caliph's feet. "Give it to me, then, Master," he said, "for I died first!" And instantly there was Nouz-Hatoul kneeling in front of the Princess, stammering out the whole story and begging for mercy for them both.

The points of the Caliph's beard gradually drooped

again and the Princess's blue eyes began to shine. A tiny silvery laugh mingled with a deeper rumbling guffaw and soon the room was full of laughing, spluttering, roaring, bellowing people – in the midst of which Abu Hassan and Nouz-Hatoul still knelt silently, awaiting their fate.

Suddenly the Caliph stopped laughing, took the curved sword from the hand of one of the guards and held it over Abu's head. A hush fell on the room as everybody waited to hear what he would say.

"I ought to slice that too-clever head from your shoulders, you rascal, but I haven't had such a laugh since you left the Court to get married. You shall have your ten thousand pieces of silver – and ten thousand pieces more each year until you really die, on condition that you both come back to live at the Palace again. We really dare not let you out of our sight from now on!"

As the procession moved back towards the Palace, the watchers outside moved away and the pigeons settled again. Soon the street was quiet once more and the little house was empty – empty, that is, except for the fly who had started it all, and he was having the feast of his life.

Tobias and the Angel

Tobit was a good man. Oh, there was no doubt about that: everybody who knew him, and especially all his relations and kinsfolk, agreed that he was a good man – and they should have known because he was always telling them so. Night and day, whoever visited the house of Tobit came away a little dazed, a little deafened, but sure of one thing, and that was that Tobit was a good man, always had been a good man and probably always would be a good man.

At the time this story begins he was in his sixty-second year and had spent most of those years helping others to a better life than the one he enjoyed himself. As a young man he had been very earnest in keeping all God's commandments. He had made all the journeys to Jerusalem that the Law prescribed. He gave one tenth of all his farm produce to the priests, and then later on he gave it to local widows and orphans. He was generous to a fault, sometimes pressing his gifts on those who did not really need them, and sometimes being tricked out of money by those who could see his weakness for a hard luck story. Since he insisted on giving a surprise gift to anyone whom he converted to the true faith, he had a remarkable number of converts to his credit – in fact it was said in the town that several disreputable men had been converted three or four times and had had the same number of gifts!

When he married, he married the daughter of a kinsman, for that was what the Law demanded, and before long they had a son, Tobias.

When Tobias was a baby, Tobit held an important position in Nineveh, with a good salary, so he was able to save a great deal of money. Wisely he deposited ten bags of silver with a cousin, Gabael, in Media, in case he should ever fall on hard times and need a reserve to fall back on. On the rest of his salary he lived well and gave generously to all who asked. In fact he prospered in Nineveh, although his tribe were not liked by the Assyrians, their captors.

However, the time came when his insistence on obeying the religious Law instead of the state law brought about his downfall. The ruler of the Assyrians was Sennacherib, who decided that the Israelites, of whom Tobit was one, were ruining the country. A cruel man, he had his soldiers round up a group of the Israelites and put them to death in the streets. Then the bodies were left to lie there; a state of affairs which horrified Tobit, for the Law said that bodies must be buried immediately. So Tobit crept out at night during these troubled times, gathered the bodies in and buried them. He tried to do it secretly, but of course someone found out and Sennacherib seized all Tobit's possessions and would have killed him if he had not taken his family into hiding. Suddenly Tobit was penniless and but for a stroke of good fortune might have remained so: two of Sennacherib's son's seized power, murdered their father and pardoned all his enemies, so Tobit and his family were able to return to their house. But of course they were now poor.

One would have thought that Tobit had learned a lesson, but he was a very good man, and it wasn't long before he was doing exactly the same thing for which he had been in trouble before. A young kinsman had been murdered by Assyrian soldiers and left in the street; Tobit sneaked out and buried him, unseen by anyone but a neighbour. This neighbour jeered at Tobit, and reminded him of what had happened before. Now this upset Tobit for the neighbour was a man whom he had helped a great deal in the past. So upset was he that he could not sleep at nights and took to lying out in the open air in the courtyard. And so it was that disaster struck, for as he lay there one night a flock of sparrows roosted on the wall overhead, and their droppings, falling on to his eyes while he slept, caused white patches which half-blinded him. Several doctors tried to cure him but all their ointments did was to make the white patches bigger, until eventually Tobit was completely blind. Anna, his wife, had to go out to work now, and it became the turn of Tobit to be on the receiving end of charity.

But Tobit was still a good man, and now that he was blind and unable to work, he found more time than ever to tell people about how well he had behaved in the past. As the years went by, young Tobias grew into a man, and often he said to his mother, Anna, "Mother, it is hard for me to say this, but I do sometimes wish that Father was not quite so good. I find it impossible to follow his example, and even more impossible to listen to his endless stories."

But Anna would quieten him, and the day came when Tobit eventually said something that really did interest Tobias.

"Anna!" he called excitedly, "Wife! What have I been thinking of? Here we are living so poorly, and you out working to keep us in food, when all the time I have lots of money!"

Anna's hands went to her mouth, and Tobit continued, "Don't you remember those ten bags of silver which I left with cousin Gabael in Media? Why, we are rich again! What a fool I am!" And he struck his brow and sent for Tobias to whom he told the whole story.

"Get ready, my son, for a journey to Rages in Media. Here is half a bill of account which Gabael and I drew up when I left the money with him. He has the other half and this will identify you as my son so that he can give you the silver."

"But Father," said Tobias doubtfully, "since I have never been out of this town in the whole of my life, how shall I find my way to our kinsman's home in Rages?"

"You must go out and find a guide," said his father after

61

some thought. "Find a good man who knows that area, and promise him a reward if he gets you there and back safely. Try to find such a man among our many relations, for our family is a good family and we can trust any of them."

So Tobias went out into the street and the very first man he bumped into happened to know the way to Rages very well. But then so he should have, for he was in fact none other than Raphael, one of God's holy angels, who had been sent down to earth to end Tobit's troubles. He had another little job to do as well, but more of that later. Well then, just as Tobias turned the key of the gate and walked into the street, there was Raphael, sitting on a low wall, and waiting to be asked.

"Media?" he said with a beaming smile. "But of course I know the way. It's a bit of luck you asked me, really, for I happen to be a kinsman of your father's – my name is Azarias, son of Ananias." Naturally he didn't want Tobias to know who he really was.

Well, there were the usual long farewells, some tears on the part of Anna, a long speech from Tobit telling the lad to be good, and a nudge or two in the ribs from Tobias's friends. But at last the boy and his companion were able to shoulder their packs, thumb their walking-sticks and take the dusty road towards Rages in Media.

Now it turned out, or rather Raphael made it turn out, that their way led by yet another of Tobit's relations, and after two days' travelling they drew near to that house. Here lived Raguel, cousin to Tobit, and Raguel had a very beautiful daughter called Sarah. It was the other part of Raphael's work on earth to see that this girl got safely married.

Raguel and Sarah lived at Ecbatana in Media, and the day before they reached that town Tobias and Raphael had to cross the River Tigris. Tobias's feet were hot and dusty, and as the two friends paddled across a ford he was kicking the water in a rainbow spray, laughing as they both got drenched. They threw themselves about in the shallows, floating and swimming and rolling under until suddenly Tobias felt his foot engulfed by the mouth of a monster fish. He screamed out loud, but Raphael stopped him, saying, "Quick, catch the fish in your hands, and heave it on to the bank."

Tobias did as he was told, and as the fish flopped and gasped on the dried mud, the Angel said, "When it is dead split it open. Take out the gall, the heart and the liver. Wrap them in cloth and keep them safely by you for they can be used as medicine." Tobias did that, and then the two lit a fire of driftwood and gorged themselves on spit-roasted steaks of fresh fish.

Eventually they arrived at the house of Raguel, and Raphael said to Tobias, "Here lives a very beautiful girl, daughter of a cousin of your father's. She would make an ideal wife for you, for she is sensible, brave, beautiful and the daughter of a very rich man. I suggest that you marry her as soon as you can; in fact I suggest that you do it before we carry on with our journey to Rages."

Well, you can imagine that Tobias was a little bit surprised at this suggestion, and he stopped dead in his tracks to think. Not that he had any objection to marrying a rich, sensible, brave and beautiful girl, but somehow at the back of his mind he sensed that there must be a snag somewhere.

"If she is so beautiful and brave and all that," he said musingly, "how is it that she is not already married?"

"Hm. Ah well, yes," said the Angel, looking just the smallest bit embarrassed. "I forgot to mention that. She *has* been married before, but her husbands happened to die on the wedding nights."

"Husbands?" said Tobias. "Nights? More than one?"

"Yes," said Raphael. "Look, here we are at Ecbatana. What a fine town!"

"Don't try to change the subject. How many more?"

"Hm. Well – er – seven actually."

"Seven! And they all died on the wedding night?"

"Afraid so, yes. As a matter of fact, there's rather a nasty old devil, a fiend, a demon – call it what you will, his name's Asmodeus – who keeps appearing every time Sarah gets married, and strangles her husbands. But you don't have to worry about him."

"No?"

"Oh, no, I assure you. Marry the girl, and then when you take her to the bridal chamber take the liver and heart of that fish that we caught and drop it on to the smoking incense which will be burning there. That will drive the demon away, I promise you."

"I should think it would drive anybody away," said Tobias, wrinkling his nose. "But are you quite sure that I shan't wake up and find myself strangled?"

"I swear it." They turned a corner and saw the house in front of them. "Now do as I say, and tomorrow Asmodeus will be gone and you will have a very young and beautiful bride."

All turned out as the Angel had said it would. Raguel liked Tobias on sight, though he was grieved to hear that his cousin Tobit had gone blind. "Such a good man," he murmured. Tobias liked Sarah, and Sarah liked Tobias. Before many hours had passed, and after a few suggestions here and there by the Angel, a marriage contract was agreed and signed, and the two young people were man and wife. Tobias was rather dazed by the speed of it all, but clutched the soggy fish package which Raphael pushed into his hand as they were led off to the bridal chamber.

Sure enough, in the middle of the night along came Asmodeus, licking his lips at the thought of his eighth victim. He came in through the window, but one sniff at the nauseous mess which was sizzling on the incense was enough to make him lay back his horns, tuck his tail between his legs and set off for Upper Egypt where he stayed for the next thousand years trying to get the smell out of his nostrils.

During the night, Raguel, who was a bit of a pessimist, made two of his servants dig a grave. "Just in case," he explained to Raphael. "The neighbours get very annoyed about all the funerals going from this house, so if by any chance the demon should happen to strangle that pleasant young man, then we can bury him swiftly. He's a stranger to the town so nobody will miss him."

Raphael smiled, but he was not too proud to join in the rejoicing, next morning, when it was discovered that Tobias was alive and well. In fact he suggested that the rejoicings should go on while he slipped over to Rages with a couple of camels and brought back Tobit's silver. Happily this was agreed and the Angel set off, at the start of a fortnight's celebrations among the bride's family.

The silver safely handed over, and Tobit's kinsman having sent all his good wishes to Tobit and Tobias, Raphael made his way back to Ecbatana. Naturally the family there wanted the young couple to stay on, but Tobias was firm.

"My father," he said, "is a good man."

"Very good," agreed Raguel.

"And he is blind also."

"Sad. Sad."

"So you see he is bound to be worrying about us. We must make all speed back home to Nineveh to tell him all our wonderful news."

So there was one last feast: many last cups of coffee were passed around, and a good many poor sheep slaughtered and eaten, but finally the little caravan of camels carrying Tobias, Sarah and Raphael set off towards Nineveh.

As they approached the city, Tobit's wife Anna, who had been watching out for them, dashed into the courtyard where Tobit was sitting and shouted out the great news.

"Tobit! Tobit! Your son is coming home with the man

you sent with him as guide. And such news! He is riding a camel hung with rich cloths and silver ornaments and he brings with him a bride, as beautiful as the morning star!"

Well, you can imagine how the old man felt about that. But there was still one more miraculous thing to happen. Just before they arrived at the house, Raphael drew Tobias aside and said, "Now, take the gall of the fish that we caught and spread it on your father's eyes, for I know that it will cure his blindness. Do as I say."

Tobias ran in to greet his father, and as they embraced he spread the fish's gall on Tobit's blind eyes. Almost at once the white patches began to melt away, so that the old man fell on his knees with joy.

"My son, my son!" he said weeping, "I can see you. My eyes are opened and I am blind no longer. Praise God!"

And as they fell on their knees to praise God, they saw that Raphael was surrounded by a shining, golden light which grew brighter and brighter until they fell on their faces in terror. And as they lay there they heard him say, "My name is Raphael. I am not one of your kinsmen, but one of the seven angels who attend the heavenly throne. Now my work on earth is finished so I can return whence I came."

The light faded and the Angel was gone, leaving a happy, rejoicing family behind him. And so all ended well, as indeed it always should for a man as good as Tobit. Yes, he really was a good man, a very good man, and he lived to be one hundred and twelve years old, during which time he was able to tell this story many, many times.

The Two Brothers

The fat, brown-skinned man sighed and wiped the sweat off his hooked nose with the back of his sleeve. The small cloud of flies that had been surrounding his camel for the last few miles rose for a second or two, and then settled again in a haze round his head. The sun continued to burn in the wide sky and the rocks on the sandy hills seemed to rise and fall as the waves of heat washed over them.

"How much farther, little rat?" he called in a good-humoured but throaty voice to the small boy who had been riding ahead and was now perched on the rump of his donkey a few yards in front, grinning back at him.

"Just over the next hill, Master Zadok. Your camel will be as pleased as you are!"

Zadok grunted, wiped his face yet again and prodded the camel into movement. The cloud of flies moved on as well.

As they breasted the last slope and began the long descent towards the huddle of buildings, surrounded by trees, which lay at the foot of the hill, Zadok saw a young man working in a deep hole near the track. The fat man reined in his camel again and shouted, and kept on shouting until the young man threw down the long-handled spade with which he had been working and climbed stiffly out of the hole.

"Is that the home of Azgad, boy?"

The youth appeared to be in a vile temper and he scowled at the merchant's words. "I am no boy. I am a man, and that is the home of Azgad, and I happen to be his son Azariah. I am only his younger son, note. If I were lucky enough to be his elder son I should not be digging this filthy well in the midday heat but lolling in the shade like my big brother

Dekar down there." He pointed and Zadok saw a small herd of cattle grazing among the trees and watched over by another young man.

"He gets fat like his cattle while I sweat my life away doing all the hard work. Who'd be a younger son, eh?"

Zadok shifted his considerable bulk on the embroidered leather of the saddle and smiled.

"Count your blessings, my young friend. I am neither a younger nor an elder son, for my father was slain by bandits before I was born and I had no cool and happy home in which to spend my young years." He urged the camel forward again leaving the young man staring after him and his swaying load of bags and parcels.

"Who is that?" Azariah asked the boy on the donkey.

"Zadok the Persian. He carries wonderful things which he has bought in markets and bazaars all over the world, and he is about to cheat your father out of some of the money which you've earned for him. Come on and watch!" And the boy slapped the donkey's rump and bobbed off after the merchant.

Visitors were rare in those days, especially such men as Zadok, so supper that evening was long and pleasant. The Persian had tales to tell in honeyed words that made Azgad and his two sons linger over their meal. The dying firelight flickered over his swarthy face, and the rings on his brown fingers flashed as his long hands helped him to describe the strange and wonderful places he had visited and the curious things he had seen.

He paused at last to sip at the tiny cup of scalding coffee and looked around at his eager listeners.

"But all my tales of travel mean nothing to you," he said. "You have here, on this farm, everything you need – family, comfort, work to keep you active and strong, food in plenty."

Azariah the younger son leaned forward. He had listened intently to Zadok's tales, especially those about the great cities

71

where there were as many people as there were ants in the tall anthill behind the old tree. He fingered the curved dagger which his father had just bought for him from the traveller, and traced the pattern stained into the leather of the hilt. If only he could leave this dry burning desert and walk in the cool shade of the city streets, see the famous bazaars where men with skins of all colours shouted and haggled with each other, bathe in the marble fountains and eat the exotic foods of the rich.

Azgad glanced at his younger son and read his mind. He looked over to where Dekar the older brother sat contentedly nodding in the sleepy firelight, and he sighed. If only Azariah and Dekar would learn to live together and work together instead of this endless jealousy and stupid bickering about who had the easier life. What would it be like when he died and the two young men had to make do without his authority, and without him to settle their quarrels? He sighed again, stretched and rose.

"God give you a good sleep, Zadok," he said. "Tomorrow we will get you to unpack your bales of cloth and perhaps come to some agreement about lightening your camel's load."

Zadok laughed as he rose to his feet. "God be with you, Azgad. My poor camel gets little relief when you feed me with such fine food as I have eaten this day. But certainly tomorrow I shall show you cobweb silks and rainbow cottons that will make the eyes of your women shine like the jewelled eyes of the Phoenix which I once saw rise like the firebird from the ruins of its own ashes . . . but that's another story."

The household went to bed, but Zadok and Azariah lingered round the dead fire, the fat man's throaty voice rising and falling as he acted out his strange stories, and the younger man sitting hunched in a blanket, with a secret resolve growing harder and harder inside his brain.

Next morning the sun had hardly begun to waken the cattle when Azariah stood before his father.

"Father, I have something to ask."

"Speak, I am listening."

"My elder brother Dekar and I are not the best of friends."

"I am not blind, my son. I have noticed."

"Father, I know he is your first-born son, and as such is entitled to more than I. But it is not my fault that I was born the year after he was, and it is not my choice that he does all the easy work around the farm while I slave away like one of the common workmen."

"I am still listening, my son."

"When you die, Father – and you know that I wish you as many years as you have hairs in your beard. . . ."

"Thank you, Son," smiled Azgad grimly, guessing what was to come.

"When you do die, Father, part of your fortune will be mine by right."

"Agreed."

"Then, Father . . ." Azariah stammered and blushed as he came to his request at last, "I should like to take my inheritance now, today, and go with Zadok to the city. Give me what would be mine on your death and let me go to find a new life, away from this desert and my lazy brother."

Azgad sat and thought. The boy was young and impetuous. But yet it *was* hard for him to be the younger son, and the brother of a man like Dekar who was quite content to work the whole of his life on the family farm. Dekar was the solid brother, but Azariah had an imagination, he had poetry in his soul, and that made it all so much harder. Perhaps it would be as well to let him go and see these things he longed for – he would go anyway as soon as his father died and it would be better to go while he was still young.

"My son," he said slowly and rose to his feet. "Take your inheritance as you call it, and may God go with you." He embraced his son, kissed him and laid his hands on his head as Azariah knelt to receive his blessing.

Zadok, pleased with his sales at Azgad's farm, agreed to escort the young man as far as the city across the great plains, and before the sun had reached its full height the two, led by the boy on the donkey, lumbered away from the farm. Azariah scarcely looked back, but Azgad and Dekar followed the travellers with their eyes until the shape of the camels blurred into the shape of the distant hills. Then they turned and got about their business, feeling almost at once that a certain life and humour had passed from the home. As Dekar said afterwards, "Although we quarrelled all the time I felt like a cow when the fly in its nostril is killed – the relief is enormous but the very fact that there is now nothing left to grumble at makes life duller and emptier."

Azariah's legs were stiff and his buttocks sore before the city was reached. For ten days he and Zadok travelled from farm to farm, and at each farm Zadok told the same stories, spreading out his silks and cotton to amaze country eyes, producing his jewelled knives and mirrors to entrance the boys and the women.

On the eleventh day, however, as they pulled into a ruined stone hut to eat and drink, Zadok pointed across the shimmering plain ahead of them with a long finger. Something white flashed in the sunlight.

"See Azariah. There are the towers of the city. Your journey is nearly over." And sure enough that very evening they passed under the gateway of the city and the dark walls closed round them.

"I will take you to an inn owned by a good friend of mine," said Zadok. "He will tell you more of this city, and advise you how to live, for tomorrow I set off again on my travels. The younger son of a rich man can afford to stay in one place, but the only son of a dead man has to move, like the finger of time, without pause."

For the first few days everything was fine. Azariah spent his money freely on all sorts of extravagances – bright clothes,

fine food and drink, a jewelled ring and a host of small and useless toys and trinkets. Everything he saw was new, bright, glittering and begging to be bought. Everyone he met wanted to sell him something. He made scores of new friends who willingly helped him to eat and drink and to spend his money. In no time at all he had got through a large part of the fortune which his father had given him, the money that had been intended to set him up for life, the money that had seemed such a vast amount back at the desert farm.

More and more money went out of Azariah's purse and none came in until at last he decided that he would have to earn more or starve. He had intended to make his living like Zadok by buying, travelling and selling, but he was too easily cheated for he knew nothing of the true worth of any kind of goods. On the other hand his own vast knowledge of the seasons, and of farm life, harvests and animals, was of no use whatsoever in the crowded city streets.

For a time he found work in the noisy bazaar, shouting out the wares for a maker of brass bowls and trays, but his voice soon got hoarse and his master kicked him out. Next he went to work for a baker on the outskirts of the city, but the heat of the tall ovens and the endless work by day and night made him ill. He lay in his little room – he had long ago had to leave the inn of Zadok's friend – and sweated in fever. By the time he was better his old job had gone and in order to buy food he had to sell his remaining few possessions, including the curved dagger that his father had bought from Zadok at their first meeting. He was penniless.

Azariah crept out of the city to the nearest farm, where he was taken on as a swineherd. But times were hard. There was famine in the land and the farmer fed his pigs first and his workers afterwards, until eventually Azariah found himself sorting through the pig-food for titbits which might keep him alive. At that very moment he knew what he wanted to do. Why should he live a life like that when on his father's farm everyone, including the poorest servant, fed well and slept comfortably? He went back to the city gate, persuaded the master of the next camel caravan going towards his father's farm to take him on as a camel-driver, and without looking back left the city behind him.

The first to spot the caravan and to recognise the younger son of the household was one of the servants. He rushed down to the farm and shouted out the news to his master, who was overjoyed at the thought of seeing again the son he had lost.

"We must celebrate," shouted Azgad. "Tell everybody to make preparations for a great feast. Go and tell Dekar the good news and ask him to kill the prize calf that he has been feeding up for just such an occasion. Tonight is a great night at this farm!"

But Dekar was not so pleased. He had said how he missed the fly in the nostril, but now that the buzzing was likely to start again he was not overjoyed at the thought.

"Father," he said in protest, "Azariah has had his inheritance. Is it fair that he should come again like this, having spent it all – and spent it all on rubbish if I know him – to beg you to take him back again? Send him away. Tell him to go back to his fine city friends. Tell him we do not want him here." And he turned away to try to hide the tears of anger.

Azgad had never seen the stolid Dekar so upset before, but he took him by the shoulders, turned him round and looked at him hard and long.

"My son," he said sympathetically. "You know how much I value you and your faithful love to me. Everthing I have is yours and will be yours after I have gone. My love to you knows no end. But, my son, Azariah has been away and we thought he was never coming back. He was dead to us and now is alive again. Be pleased to see him, for he is your brother and my son."

Dekar looked over his father's shoulder and suddenly Azariah was in the doorway, sunken-eyed from the fever, pale and thin from the city life, his face downcast in shame, and tears making long furrows in the red dust on the lean face. Dekar put his father aside and strode over to his younger brother. He lifted his arm and put it round the boy's shoulders, kissed him and led him to a bench near the table. Then he turned and shouted for a servant: "Fetch warm water and oil so that I can wash my brother's feet. Bring the softest cloths for me to dry them." And Dekar stooped, and washed, and anointed, and no one saw the tears in his own eyes.

The
Divided Horsecloth

Old Paul was getting very old. His son, Pierre, said so in a voice that held a mixture of sadness and irritation; he said so very often to his wife Jeanne who agreed, in a voice that was all irritation and no sadness. Old Paul, hearing Jeanne's shrill voice as it penetrated the filigree plaster ceiling of the dining-room, the polished split pine floors of the main bedrooms, and the plain unvarnished planks of the attic where he slept, shivered and drew his moth-eaten fur cloak closer round his bony ankles. Yes, the world was left in no doubt when Jeanne spoke: Old Paul was getting very old.

"I'm getting old, Jacques," said Old Paul one day to his only grandson who was sitting on the broad stone window-sill of the old man's attic bedroom, gazing out over the lush river valley. The boy turned back from the view outside, and pitched a well-chewed apple core into the smoky fireplace. He looked over at his grandfather and smiled with affection.

"Yes, I know, Grandfather," he said. "You're getting older. And so is my father. And so am I. Old age starts the day we are born and nothing we can do or say will make it come any more slowly."

Old Paul nodded and smiled, but deep down inside himself he was worried. There had been something astir in the house over the past few months, some hidden menace that foreshadowed bad things to come. He got up slowly out of his chair and crossed to the window to put one hand on the boy's shoulder. The two gazed out across the countryside which had a white dusting of snow from the previous day's east wind. Down below a peasant hurried a

cart-load of wood from the forest to the shelter of the town walls, anxious to get there before night fell.

"I remember," said Old Paul, "when I was a young man, and had just bought this house. . . ." His thoughts roamed back over the years and he saw himself again, a plump young merchant, proud of his pretty wife and looking forward to the birth of a son. Ah, yes, those were the days, when he was on the way up, when everything he touched turned to gold. In those days his ships sailed out of the harbour for the Northlands to bring back furs and sealskins, and for the Holy Land to bring back spices, carried overland from those magic countries east of the sun. He had been lucky in his strong ships and honest captains, and they in their turn had been lucky in staying clear of pirates, shipwrecks and the strange beasts which mariners said lurked in the distant oceans. All had gone well and his oak chests had groaned with the weight of the golden profits from his merchant ventures.

Old Paul smiled as he remembered how proud he had been when his son Pierre was born. His young wife, too, had laughed all day and they took delight in making the new nursery room bright and cheerful with soft hangings, deep skin rugs and brightly painted furniture. Pierre had been a good baby and had grown tall and strong and fearless, a keen horse-rider and proficient in the use of longbow and singlestick. He had coursed hares with the sons of other merchants, and had even gone in for hawking, a sport usually reserved for the nobility.

And then – Old Paul stirred and shivered as he remembered – his pretty young wife had died. She had taken a chill one Christmas while watching the birth of a foal to her prize Arab mare. The chill had turned to a fever, and in spite of the constant care of the physicians and the use of the finest leeches from the banks of the Loire, her beautiful face had grown gaunt, her fair hair had straightened and she had died. Paul was heart-broken and had vowed to remember her always. The love which he had given to her was turned completely to his son Pierre, and his main ambition became a desire to see that Pierre became a rich and powerful man.

Pierre had already shown interest in his father's business, and by the time he was of marriageable age he was beginning to be known throughout the district as one prepared to take risks, but one also with all the luck in the world on his side. Paul was justly proud of the son he had reared, and the son was equally proud of his father.

Nearby, in a chateau on the edge of the sea, there had lived a nobleman with a daughter, Jeanne. Noblemen usually married off their daughters to the sons of noble friends, but this particular lord was short of money. His scrappy vineyards had suffered three bad blights in three years; he had spent a lot of his capital on the upkeep of the chateau and he had wasted a lot more on extravagant parties and costume balls for his richer friends. Paul, a good business man, knew that the lord needed money badly and so he eyed the daughter Jeanne, a girl with a long nose and a sulky look, as a possible wife for his son Pierre.

The arrangements had been long drawn-out. Paul had had to be cunning, careful and patient but at last he and the lord came to an agreement. Jeanne would be given to Pierre as his wife. She would bring no dowry, since the knight had nothing to give anyway, but she would bring the title, breeding and connections of the ancient family. In return Paul agreed to hand over immediately all his business to Pierre. Everything was to be given to the son: the business, the capital, the ownership of the trading vessels and warehouses, even the very house itself in which they would all live. Pierre would become head of the family at once while he, Paul, would spend his remaining years in retirement, happy in the knowledge that he had arranged a good match for his son.

But it had not worked out quite like that. Jeanne had been a good wife and obedient, and then before long there had been the little grandson for everyone to admire. But as the years went by Jeanne had begun to grow tired of having Old Paul constantly round the house. Her nose seemed to grow sharper and her expression more sulky still. She longed for a time when the old man would not be there, needing attention, telling his boring old stories to their smart friends, spoiling his grandson with sweetmeats and unsuitable gifts. She began to complain to Pierre about his father, and gradually Old Paul found himself being left out of family gatherings; his belongings were moved into fresh rooms higher and higher in the house until he was in the cheerless attic; his clothes got older and more ragged and he was given no money to renew them. By the time young Jacques' voice was breaking, Old Paul had become a drag on the household and was pushed around by the meanest of the servants.

All these thoughts went sadly through Old Paul's head, but still he did not regret his decision to arrange Pierre's marriage to Jeanne. Twelve years had failed to change his mind, though his life was but a shadow of what it had been. He turned away from the window and went over to the fire to warm his bony ankles.

"Jacques!" The voice from down below was unmistakably Jeanne's and both the old man and the boy started guiltily. "Jacques! If you're up there with your grandfather, come down immediately. I've told you before, I will not have you up there listening to that stuff and nonsense."

"Good-night, Grandfather," said the boy. "Tomorrow I will catch a rabbit with the snare you made for me, and you and I will stew it on your little fire." He kissed the old man and went off downstairs where Jeanne's shrill voice could be heard greeting him.

Old Paul lit a tallow candle and prepared for bed. But before he could climb into his sagging cot he had a surprise visit from his son Pierre. Pierre was uncomfortable about what he had to say, and he could not look his father in the eye. While the old man sat on the edge of the bed, he marched up and down the attic stammering out the words slowly as though he were ashamed to let his father hear them.

"Father, it's like this. We have had you living in our house now for twelve years, and my wife Jeanne is tired. She is tired of having you around all the time, tired of seeing you ordering her servants about, tired of watching you spoil our son Jacques."

Old Paul drew his cloak round his knees and waited anxiously for the rest. He had learned to be patient over the past few years but he half-guessed what was to come.

"Go on, my son," he said. "Say what you have to say."

"I'm sorry, Father, but tomorrow you must go."

"Go? But where should I go to?"

"Anywhere. Out of this house. Go and seek home and shelter elsewhere. Twelve years is too long for us to have to feed and keep you."

Old Paul stretched out a thin hand. "But there is nowhere I can go to, my son. I have no friends now who would take me in. I must stay here."

"You cannot stay here. I have told you. Jeanne and I have decided. You must go down into the town and seek the company of other old men. Perhaps when you get there you will find your fortune and will be able to start a new life."

"You know that I am too old to start a new life, Pierre, and how should an old man find a fortune? Will you please have pity on me and let me stay?"

"No, Father, you must go. Ask for shelter in the town. Someone will take you in."

"Who will take me in? I have nothing to give in exchange. To you I gave everything I had, and if you will not give me food and shelter how can I expect anyone else to do so?"

Pierre walked to the door, his face flushed with

85

embarrassment. "Nevertheless, Father, tomorrow you must go. Jeanne and I have decided." The oak door creaked open and shut and he was gone.

The next morning dawned grey and cheerless. A thin mist lay heavily over the little town and the leafless trees dripped water constantly on to muddy pathways. Somewhere a dog was howling mournfully.

Old Paul had not slept. During the night, after praying for guidance, he had gathered his few belongings into a small bundle, counted his last few coins into a shabby purse, and wrapped himself in as many clothes as he had. Yet still he felt cold in the morning air and he shivered violently as he felt his way downstairs to the kitchen.

Old Mercy the cook gave him a bowl of thin gruel, which he drank gratefully, sucking the hot oats over his aching gums. He thought bitterly of what the coming night would be like for it seemed to him that he would probably have to sleep in a barn or even in the open air. Suddenly he had a thought.

"Son," he said to Pierre who with Jeanne was standing grimly in the doorway, "give me one last thing. Your horse will be better off than I from now on, for he will at least sleep in a warm stable with fresh straw daily, yet he has also a warm horsecloth. Will you give me that horsecloth to keep my old bones warm at night?"

Pierre hesitated for a second then called for his son Jacques to go and fetch the cloth. The boy was soon back carrying the heavy cloth, but instead of handing it straight to his grandfather he drew the hunting knife from his belt, held the cloth up and slashed it in half from top to bottom. Comparing the two halves, he folded one up and gave it to his grandfather while he tucked the other piece up under his own arm.

Old Paul's eyes at last filled with tears at this final piece of unkindness. He turned slowly towards the door but stopped as Pierre began to shout at the boy.

"How dare you do that!" he yelled. "I told you to give him the whole cloth, and yet you took back half of it!"

The boy turned to face his father and looked him squarely in the eyes. "Father," he said, "you have brought me up well, and have shown me how to make the best out of life and, above all, how to win in life. I have watched you, and seen how you have gradually taken from Grandfather everything he ever had. I have much admired the way you have left him penniless, and now homeless, by turning him out of his own house."

Pierre started to speak but the boy continued in a flat voice. "Father, you have taught me all this and I am grateful. When I am a grown man I shall be able to follow your example. This piece of horsecloth I have kept back, so that I shall have something to give to you when it is your turn to be thrown out into the cold."

Nobody moved for a while, and then Pierre strode over to the old man and putting his arm round his shoulders led him to a seat by the fire. Then he turned to Mercy the cook.

"Go and light a fire in the best guest-room, and prepare it as my father's room. Then cook him a good big breakfast, while I find warm clothes from my press which will last him until the little tailor in the town can make him new ones. Go."

The woman bustled out of the room, and the long-nosed Jeanne, who had started to say something and then stopped, also went out shamefaced.

"Father," said Pierre, "I am very ashamed and very sorry. It took my young son to teach me a lesson which I richly deserved. For the rest of your life you shall live with us as an honoured guest, eating and drinking whatever you want, and wearing the finest clothes, as befits a man of your position. Never will I forget today, however, and as a constant reminder of my foolishness I intend to prepare an empty space on the wall of the room where I sleep, and there I shall hang the divided horsecloth as a reminder of what I nearly did."

The Whistling Butcher

The butcher's real name doesn't matter because everybody called him Whistler. He had a habit of whistling as he drove his rickety cart from market to market, only pausing to shout in a wailing voice the one word, "Meat!" every time he stopped. He was in fact a man of very few words. His wife, who was fat and cheerful, swore that when he was at home with her he was never quiet, but outside his little house he was known only as Whistler.

It really was a beautiful morning and Whistler could be forgiven for trying to outdo the birds as he jogged along through the middle of Sherwood Forest towards Nottingham for the mid-week market. A warm summer sun burned down through the spreading leaves of the oak trees and the grass underfoot was green and soft. As the cart rumbled down the bank of a stream and across a shallow ford, the cool water sluicing between his toes made Whistler feel life was great, life was marvellous. He pursed his lips, imitating the clear call of a blackbird, and caught at the bridle on his horse's head to help him up the opposite bank.

However, as he breasted the slope the whistle died in his throat, and he coughed nervously. A man was sitting in the middle of the track, holding a long yew-bow across his knee and whittling away at the shaft of an arrow. The morning suddenly seemed less beautiful, the sun seemed cooler and Whistler realised that his feet were wet, he was in the middle of a lonely forest and Nottingham was a long way away.

The stranger looked up. He was tanned brown by an outdoor life, and his clothes were the colour of the trees and bushes. A short sword hung from his deerskin belt and there was a long quarterstaff on the ground close by. The man had the air of one who was used to getting his own way, and already in Whistler's mind dim guesses were beginning to form as to who he might be.

"Meat?" said Whistler in a thin voice. The man laughed, and in one lithe movement was on his feet and standing by the horse's nose at Whistler's side.

"No meat," said the stranger. He rapped with the quarterstaff on the wheels of the cart, idly playing a tune on the spokes as he peered at the sides of beef, legs of mutton and half-pigs neatly arranged on the bottom boards. Suddenly there was a flash as the short sword swung up and down again and the stranger was holding a pig's tail in his hand. He laughed again.

"You going to Nottingham, butcher?" he asked, prowling round past the tail-board, idly swinging the curly pink tail from his fingers.

"Yes," said Whistler, hopefully.

"Do you know me?"

"I've a pretty good idea who you might be," said Whistler, quite sure who his new acquaintance was.

The stranger brought the hand holding the pig's tail up until the curl was swinging backwards and forwards in front of the frightened butcher's eyes.

"Well, go on then, tell me. Who am I?"

"People call you, I think, Master – er – people call you Robin Hood."

"So. And what do people call you?"

The butcher swallowed. "Some folk call me Whistler, Master."

Robin Hood put his lean brown face close to the butcher's white, sweaty one.

"Then listen to me, Whistler. And listen carefully. What is this?"

"Pig's tail," said Whistler.

"Not much use to anyone," said Robin. "Neither is the pig's squeal. And neither will you be if ever you tell anyone what I am going to say, for if you do I shall cut you into little curly pieces the size of that tail, and dig the last squeal out of you with this sword." Whistler felt a sudden sharp pinprick in his thigh and backed away in alarm.

"I never talk," he said, falling to his knees. "Never. I am known for never talking. All I ever say is 'Meat'."

Robin Hood stepped back from the grovelling butcher and took from his green tunic a small doeskin purse which jingled in his hand. He pulled back the draw-string and emptied on to the grass a little stream of golden coins, each one flashing in the sun as it fell.

"See how much there is there, butcher," said Robin.

Whistler fumbled with trembling fingers to pick the coins out of the short grass. They were wet from the morning dew.

"There's more money than I have ever seen," he said at last.

"It's yours, then. Take it. Just leave behind your horse, your cart, your meat and that foul black smock that you are wearing."

Whistler pulled off the smock quickly enough, bent again with a grunt to pick up the rest of the coins, took a last look at the man who would pay so much for so little and set off at a trot towards home. As he splashed through the ford he heard the rumble of the wheels as Robin Hood drove away.

There had been no need to tell Whistler twice to keep his mouth shut. He had heard of too many men who just disappeared into Nottingham Castle never to emerge again, just because it was thought they might know something about the Sherwood outlaws. Tongues could be torn out at roots, and although he did not talk a lot, he didn't particularly want to be prevented from talking at all. In fact it was years before he told even his wife how it was that he had returned early from market one day without his smock and cart but with a small fortune in gold.

Meanwhile Nottingham Market was well under way by the time Robin Hood arrived there with his cart-load of meat. The dirty cobbled square was full of yelling merchants, gold-toothed cheapjacks and the usual milling crowd of townspeople looking for cheap food and bargains. The butcher in black reined up his cart in a narrow space by the side of a man selling cheese and butter. He dropped the tail-board, climbed on to the cart and yelled, "Meat! Who'll buy my meat!"

The seller of cheeses looked across at him. "Where's Whistler?" he said shortly.

"Sold up," said the butcher. "I've taken over his pitch. Meat! Who'll buy my meat!"

A round, fat woman carrying a rush basket and dragging three screaming children behind her, came to the cart and looked in. She poked a grimy finger-nail into one of the joints and sniffed disdainfully.

"Usual poor stuff," she said, picking up a small joint of lamb and brushing a fly off it. "How much for this scrag-end?"

The butcher took the piece of meat off her and inspected it, weighing it in his hands professionally. Then he picked up another, bigger piece, put the two together and offered her both for a farthing.

"What did you say?" said the woman in astonishment and even the children stopped screaming as if they couldn't believe their ears.

They're both yours for a farthing," said Robin. "Take them or leave them."

The woman grabbed them, handed over a coin and disappeared into the crowd, chattering excitedly to passers-by as she did so. The word spread like wildfire that a madman was practically giving away meat, and the cart became surrounded by would-be buyers. The cheese seller next door had his stall pushed over, the rumpus grew and soon the cart stood like a rock in the middle of a sea of upturned faces and waving arms. Nottingham Market had never seen anything like it.

Over by the stone horse-trough, a gift from the last Sheriff but one, a small squad of the Sheriff's soldiers lounged and scratched and spat and guffawed. They were really there on duty to keep order in the market and to watch out for cutpurses and common thieves, but it was a long time since they had had to do anything more than arrest a known villain or throw out a beggar. However, on this day, it gradually came to their notice that something unusual was going on over in the corner by the church. They grabbed hastily for their weapons and set off at a slow run towards the centre of the disturbance. Arriving where the crowd was thickest they formed a wedge shape and using fists, shields, feet and elbows drove their way to the side of the cart where the mad butcher had just sold a whole pig for a penny. The leader of the men-at-arms jumped up on to the cart, drew his sword, scowled at the crowd and put one hand on the mad fellow's shoulder.

"Arrested!" he yelled and the crowd bayed in anger. Hands holding out coins became fists shaking and for a moment it looked as if the mob would overturn the cart and just take the meat anyway. But the soldiers were well trained. At a word they too drew their swords, formed up round the cart and presented their shields and grim faces to those trying to get closer. The crowd fell back muttering and the little procession rumbled away towards Nottingham Castle, followed by curses and not a few old cabbage stalks.

The news got to the Castle before the cart did for the portcullis was up and the gates were wide open. Whistler's old horse plodded slowly into the courtyard and stopped to graze at a patch of grass growing through the slabs. A

splendid figure in cloth of gold now emerged from an archway and came down a short flight of stone steps to greet them.

"So," said this magnificent person, who Robin recognised as the Sheriff. "So this is the mad butcher who sells cheap meat. Let's have a look at him." The soldiers dragged Robin off the cart and pushed him forward in front of the Sheriff. Robin bent his back and grinned vacantly.

"My Lord?" he said.

"Are you mad, fellow?"

"I sell meat, my Lord."

"But you are not a butcher. Your voice is not rough, and I would guess you are well-born, if a little stupid. And you sell meat far too cheaply. You are either a knave or you are mad. Perhaps a taste of the thumbscrew will tell us which."

Robin bent forward and said in a low voice so that only the Sheriff could hear, "My Lord, I am not mad nor am I a knave. I sell the meat cheaply because it costs me nothing." He stepped back again.

The Sheriff gestured the soldiers to stand back out of earshot and then went forward himself. "If it costs you nothing, then I suppose you steal it?"

"No, my Lord. Thank you for listening to me in private, my Lord, for I would not wish everyone to know what I know I can trust you with."

"Go on."

"You see, my Lord Sheriff, I live on my father's estates, and his animals are numbered in thousands."

"Ah, I see, your father is a rich man?"

"You might almost say he is the richest man in this kingdom."

"And he has a lot of animals?" said the Sheriff.

"Thousands of fine beasts, my Lord. More than he knows what to do with. All grazing on vast areas of good land."

"So you take a few beasts and sell them cheaply – and he never finds out?"

"He is away, my Lord Sheriff, at the Crusades, but were he here he would not grudge me the few that I take."

The Sheriff thought, and it was a greedy thought. "I see. I see. Well now, would you care to sell me a few of those fine beasts?"

"Yes, of course, my Lord, give me the money now and I will bring them to you."

The Sheriff laughed. "Oh no, my fine fellow, that's not the way I do business. I shall come with you to see what I am buying, and so I shall be able to say how many and which ones I will buy."

The butcher said, "If you come with me I will show you animals such as you would never believe existed in this shire. But you must come alone, for I shall show the herds to no one apart from you. You I can trust, but who else is to be trusted these days?"

The Sheriff hesitated, but not for long. He eyed the figure in the dirty black smock, looked hard at the vacant, simple face and decided to take the risk. Here was a simpleton who stole from his absent father, and as soon as the Sheriff had found out where these great herds of beasts were then he could imprison the thief and find some way to confiscate the cattle. He smiled to himself; many lords and barons had gone off to the Crusades and returned to find themselves penniless.

"Agreed," he said shortly, then turned and called for his horse. Mounting, he followed the creaking cart out through the Castle gate, drawing a scarf across his face to shield himself from recognition.

Once out of the city the butcher whipped up the horse into a smart trot and they soon began to draw near to the tall trees of Sherwood Forest. The Sheriff felt a little shiver run up his spine as he thought of the outlaws living there, so he clapped his heels into the horse's side to bring him level with the butcher.

97

"How far must we go?" he called, panting with the exertions of the ride on such a warm day.

"Almost there," said the butcher. They entered the forest and a few minutes later reached a grassy clearing, at the other side of which were grazing about twenty magnificent roe-deer.

"See," said the butcher, "the first of my father's herds."

For a minute the Sheriff was speechless. His first thought was that the young man was, after all, mad, but then he noticed something else in the clearing as well as the deer. A man in green clothes was lying quite still in the dappled shadow of a tree; he looked again, and saw another idly resting one elbow against an oak; a third man now appeared, or perhaps he had been there all the time, sitting by a gorse bush. All were armed.

The Sheriff started to turn his horse, but a big man had hold of the bridle and he could not move, so he just sat still and waited, cursing the greed which had got him into this situation. He didn't need to be told now who the butcher really was.

Robin peeled off the black smock, and within minutes the Sheriff was sitting on a tussock of warm grass watching while large chunks of venison from some hidden larder, hung to perfection and roasted on spits over the glowing embers of a small fire, were carved and handed round. At first he refused to eat but then the big man sat beside him and although he said nothing his eyes glowed darkly, so that the Sheriff thought it wise to take what was offered.

The venison was hot, spiced with herbs and rich with juices, and the bread they ate with it was fresh-baked and wholesome. The men ate quietly, watching their leader who was obviously enjoying his meal. At last the Sheriff could bear the silence no longer.

"Liar," he said quietly.

"No liar, my Lord," said Robin, equally quietly.

"You said that you were a butcher."

"And so I was, for a day. The cart and goodwill had been well paid for."

"You said your father owned these herds, and yet they turn out to be the King's deer."

"And is not the King my father? And your father? And the father of all his countrymen? I told you that he was rich and away at the Crusades. I told you that he owned vast areas of land. Could you not have guessed who I meant? Or did greed blind your common sense?" Robin threw a chewed bone into the fire and stretched.

"You can pay for your supper now," he said.

"You will get nothing from me," said the Sheriff boldly, but again the big man came close, and it was a subdued Sheriff who handed over both his purses, the small one at his belt and the other, bigger one from the secret pocket inside his gown.

"Thief!" said the angry Sheriff.

"Just payment," said Robin. "Payment for your supper, and perhaps for some of the suppers of the hundreds of people round Nottingham who have been robbed by your unjust taxes."

The Sheriff could find nothing to say. His clothes were sticking to him with sweat, and he just wanted to get away.

"Bring his horse," said Robin, and a man led forward the horse, which had had its rich saddle and accoutrements removed. The Sheriff started to say something, but then had second thoughts. He caught the horse by its mane and swung himself up on to its back with an ease that showed him to be a soldier in spite of everything. One of the outlaws raised his staff to give the horse a thwack on its rump but Robin stopped him.

"Master Sheriff," he said, looking up at the Sheriff's tight mouth and narrowed eyes. "King Richard will be back in England before long. Why not give up your evil oppression

of the poor and break off your friendship with Prince John? The King appointed you to a rich and trustworthy office, and you could still do it well if you wished."

The Sheriff bared his teeth and laughed. "Goodbye, fellow. The next time I see you, you will either be in chains or dead. And I shall have your skin flayed from your flesh, stretched on wood, inscribed with a message and sent to your King Richard in the Holy Land, telling him what fine friends he has in England. And telling him what dead men they are too!"

He eased himself on to the neck of the horse and trotted out of the clearing with a straight back. Robin grinned, shrugged and wandered back to where the others were dozing and chatting. He sat on the grass, cross-legged, and began whittling at the shaft of an arrow while the rising evening wind blew a cold breeze through his thin clothes.

Till Eulenspiegel and the Inn-Keeper

The Inn at Eisleben stood tall in the village, its black and white timber jutting out like the prow of a ship over the thatched roofs of the surrounding cottages. Thick snow had put an iced layer over the rough cobbled streets and the raw winds blowing across the plains from the east made sure that few of the villagers would venture out that night.

Inside the Inn, however, a great fire, fed with logs of sweet-smelling pine and birch roared in the open hearth, sending a warm glow to the ordered rows of pewter tankards on the dresser shelves. Claus, the landlord, was a burly man with a pallid face and huge mottled arms. His temper was unsure and he could be quite unpleasant to villagers and travellers alike when he felt like it, picking on their weaknesses and making them look foolish in front of their friends. It really was a wonder that anyone stayed at his Inn, but then it was the only one in the village and his wife was a splendid cook, so folk generally put up with his jibes for the sake of a soft bed and good food.

Claus banged a wooden shutter over the last of the windows and dropped the square bolt securely into place. He wiped his fat hands on a coarse linen apron and shouted to his wife in the kitchen, "Is that roast beef done yet?"

His wife, a flustered little women with a smudge of flour on her cheek, peered through the door at him. "Just a few minutes, husband, the boy . . ."

"I'll kick that boy out into the snow if he's fallen asleep over the spit again!"

"No, husband, don't be so hasty. I was just going to say that he's basting the roast for the last time. Five minutes, Claus, and no longer, I promise you."

She disappeared and Claus spat into the fire, making the logs hiss. Every night was the same, he thought, never food just when he wanted it. He could do the job far better and more quickly himself, but then what did he keep a wife for if not to cook? So he shrugged his shoulders and waited, reflecting that after all with the snow so bad and the wind so keen there might well be nobody to eat the meat but himself. Scarcely the night for travellers, and all the better if there were none. His mouth began to water and he licked his thick lips at the thought of the great slices of sizzling red meat and yellow fat which he would soon be carving.

Even at the thought there was a loud bang at the front door. He strode over and lifted the latch, peering out into the white swirl of the night. Suddenly, from the kitchen came a scream. Leaving the door ajar he rushed to see what was the matter.

"A face!" said his wife, pointing at the window, and the boy nodded violently. "A great, grinning, ugly face with a long waving white beard!"

Claus started to tell her not to be so stupid when all at once he heard another loud thump from the front. With an oath he rushed back to the front door, slammed it shut and hammered the bolt home with one blow of his fist.

He stepped back and began to breathe more easily, and then almost jumped out of his skin as he felt a light tap on his shoulder. Heart beating wildly he whirled round to find a smallish man, with a cheerful red face, swathed in a very long coat, smiling and nodding at him.

"Evening, Landlord," said the little man. "I couldn't make anyone hear at the front so I went round to the back and looked in at the window. But all I could see there were two people making funny faces at me so I came back to the front.

And there I was just wiping my boots on the mat when all of a sudden you appeared yourself like a hunted boar and started slamming bolts all over the place. What's the matter with you all?"

The landlord was recovering from his shock a little, and couldn't help feeling that the visitor was not quite as innocent as he made out.

The little man had taken off his long coat to reveal another one underneath. He handed the first which was wet with snow to Claus and introduced himself while he started to take off the second. "How-d'ye-do. My name's Eulenspiegel, but since most people can't get their tongues round that very easily, you can call me Till."

The second coat was handed over.

"But my wife said that the face at the window had got a great white beard."

Till nodded at the floor where lay a long white scarf. "Perhaps she saw that?" he suggested, and handed the landlord yet another coat. Claus began to laugh and the little man laughed, and the landlord's wife laughed, and even the boy began to laugh until Claus hit him such a blow on the ear that he nearly fell into the dripping tin.

"Supper!" roared Claus, rubbing his hands.

"Supper," agreed Till, taking off his last overcoat.

But even then they had to wait a little, for there was another knocking and three more travellers arrived out of the snow and ice, stamping their boots and full of stories about the blackness of the forest and the ferocity of the local wolves.

"Only half an hour from here," said one of the travellers, "we actually saw some of the beasts."

"It was very frightening," said another. They told how a great black wolf had sprung on to the track out of the forest, had faced them with a snarl, and had looked as if it would attack them.

Claus spat into the fire. "What did you do then?" he asked contemptuously.

"Why, nothing!" said the first traveller. "We were so frightened that we just stood there looking at it, and at last it gave a terrible howl and slunk off into the forest again."

Till murmured sympathetically, but the landlord was full of scorn.

"What?" said Claus, forking big helpings of beef and turnips into his gaping mouth, "three of you – and frightened of just one wolf! Why, many's the time when I've been on my own, and I've just shouted at whole packs of the cowardly things and watched them run away in fear. I could grapple bare-handed with two at a time if I tried but they daren't get anywhere near me. They soon get to know who's afraid and who isn't." And he lifted his ham-like fist and flexed the great rolling fat of his arm.

For the rest of the meal Claus continued to poke fun at the three travellers until they were sorry they had ever stopped there, and even Till was glad to get away from him and go to bed. They were taken upstairs to the small, lamplit attic room which all four visitors were to share. As they quickly slipped out of their outer clothes and got in between the rough twill of the sheets, exclaiming at the cold, Till spoke to his three companions.

"Look," he said, "that Claus is a pretty obnoxious sort of chap. Would you like to see him taken down a peg or two?"

"That we would," they said enthusiastically.

"Very well, then, I will arrange it. In a week's time we will all meet again at this Inn. By that time I shall have something ready that will make Master Landlord's boasting disappear like this –" and with a quick puff he blew out the candle and fell fast asleep.

One week later to the day he was back at the Inn carrying something cold and stiff in a large sack. The three travellers were there as well and again Claus was taking delight in

106

reminding them of how cowardly they had been, and how he would have torn the wolf apart with his bare hands.

Till and the three travellers went up to their bedroom early, but stayed dressed until they heard Claus also come up to bed. Then Till lugged his heavy sack from under his bed and emptied it on to the floor. Out fell the stiffened body of a large black wolf which he himself had hunted down and killed the day before. Silently he crept downstairs to the kitchen, laid the dead wolf out on the hearthrug and placed one of the maid's wooden shoes between its hideous teeth. Then he went back to the bedroom and nodded to his friends. Immediately they started to shout and sing and hammer on the wall.

"Landlord!" they called. "We feel like drinking. Send someone downstairs for a large can of ale for each of us. Hurry up!"

Claus was annoyed at this for he had just climbed into his night-shirt. He didn't intend going back downstairs for anyone so he, in turn, yelled for the serving-girl and sent her for the drinks. The four visitors waited, grinning, to see what would happen.

They had not long to wait. They heard the soft slap of the maid's bare feet going down the wooden staircase, then the groaning creak of the kitchen door, then silence.

"One, two, three, four . . ." counted Till.

As he reached the count of five there was an ear-splitting screech, a terrific bang of the back door and then a series of yells getting fainter and fainter as the girl disappeared towards her mother's cottage in the village.

After a while, the three travellers again hammered on the wall. "Landlord, what about our drinks?"

Claus was very annoyed by now. He had not heard the serving-girl and had believed that she had served their guests and gone back to bed. So he had to get out of bed and yell down the corridor at the pot-boy who slept under the stairs.

"Hans!" he shouted. "Fetch ale for our visitors. I told Gretchen to go but she must have fallen asleep again."

The four travellers listened again. They heard the grunts of the pot-boy as he grumbled and shambled towards the kitchen, the groaning creak of the kitchen door, and then silence.

"One, two, three, four . . ." counted Till.

As he reached the count of five there was a hoarse whistling kind of shout as the boy shot like greased lightning out of the kitchen and down the cellar steps to hide among the barrels.

After a while, the travellers hammered on the wall for a third time.

"Landlord!" they yelled. "What kind of an inn is this? Twice we have called for ale and for all the service we've had you might as well all be dead. Fetch us some ale at once, do you hear?"

This time Claus had no one else to send, so out he went in his night-shirt and slippers to do the travellers' bidding. The four men hugged themselves with delight as they heard him slip-slop downstairs, then the groaning creak of the kitchen door, then silence.

"One, two, three, four . . ." counted Till.

On the count of five there began a long low howl from down below. It began soft and then got louder and louder, and at the same time there was a strange drumming sound like castanets. The noise got nearer and nearer until suddenly the bedroom door burst open and there stood the brave Claus, white as flour, howling with fear and teeth chattering fit to wake the dead.

Till stepped forward and slapped his face, leaving four scarlet finger marks on one cheek. But it stopped him screaming and chattering, and he fell on his knees weeping.

"Oh, help, help, help!" he sobbed. "Downstairs in the kitchen – sob – is the biggest wolf you ever saw – sob –

and it's roaming round roaring – sob – and it's already eaten the boy and it's just swallowed – sob – the girl's left foot. Please come and kill it for me. Please!"

"What?" said Till, "can this be the man who could tear two wolves to pieces with his bare hands if only they could come close enough?" And he took Claus by one ear, led him unwillingly downstairs and showed him the dead wolf with the shoe in its mouth.

The landlord was rather quiet for a time after that night, especially as the girl had brought folk back from the village to see the wolf. They spared him nothing, and their remarks and those of the boy and of his own wife made him a quieter, kinder man from then on.

As for Till and the travellers they never got their ale. But they had a very good night's entertainment, and they slept soundly until morning in their beds at the Inn at Eisleben.

Jovinian's Nightmare Day

The early morning sun was beginning to melt away the white mists which surrounded the Emperor Jovinian's palace as he looked out of his bedroom window. Today was the day when he had promised himself a good gallop on his new stallion, hunting deer. Yes, the sun was going to be hot and it would be good to get among the cool trees in the shady forest.

Jovinian stretched, yawned and began to dress. Silent servants handed him his clothes, but the Emperor himself was far from silent. He sang as he fastened buckles, tied strings and ran podgy fingers through his grizzled hair. Still singing he strode over to the full-length polished bronze mirror and admired his imperial reflection.

"Good morning, Jovinian," he said to himself. "How fortunate you are to be an emperor on such a fine morning. Here you are, rich, powerful, handsome, lord of all you can see. Your people respect and love you, even worship you, for to them you are like a god. In fact, which god could be so strong, so mighty and yet so wise? Which god ever did so much for mankind?" He smoothed the pure white tunic over his rather fat stomach and took another self-satisfied look at his reflection in the mirror.

"Yes, I am like a god," he said. "No, let's face it, I *am* a god. Is there, in fact, any other god but me? Perhaps I am the one and only true god."

And so, reflecting on this thought, he set off for his day's hunting riding his new stallion so fiercely that in spite of the shade of the forest trees both rider and horse were soon

hot and sweaty. The chase led to a small, reed-skirted lake at which the horse could drink. A brace of wild duck took off from the surface as Jovinian approached and spattered silver drops from their paddle feet as they flew away over the trees. A smoky grey heron stepped delicately out of the shallows, seemed to lift effortlessly into the air and flapped away. A heat haze shimmered at the far end of the lake, and Jovinian was tempted to bathe. No sooner thought than done and throwing his clothes over a fallen tree-trunk he told his followers to ride on and that he would catch them up. Almost before they were out of sight, Jovinian was up to his waist in the green water and then swimming with a long trolling stroke out towards the centre.

The water was really very cold at its deepest part, and despite the hot sun Jovinian was shivering as he picked his way through the marsh marigolds to where he had left his clothes. He thought with pleasure of the short ride ahead to the home of a friend where they were all to have a meal before riding back in the afternoon to his palace.

But then he had a shock. His clothes had disappeared and his beautiful horse was nowhere to be seen. Someone must have crept up while he was swimming and stolen them. A black scowl settled on the Emperor's face as he padded in bare feet round the tree-trunk. What was to be done now? He called out at the top of his voice, but his followers were long out of earshot. There he was in the forest, all alone and as naked as the day he was born. There was nothing for it but to start walking to his friend's house where, no doubt, he would soon be given clean clothes and a horse.

Jovinian's pink feet were not made to trample through mud and over sharp twigs and snaggly thorns. By the time he reached the outer door of his friend's house his feet were black, cut and very sore, while his temper was also black and very nearly ready to explode.

He knocked, and when there was no immediate answer

he raised both fists and hammered on the nailed oak. From inside came a shuffling noise and then with a creak and a groan the heavy door swung open to show the face of the gatekeeper, astonished at the spectacle of a naked man. Jovinian started to walk through the gateway but was stopped by a hairy hand placed flat on his royal chest.

"Now then," said the gatekeeper. "Where do you think you're going, fellow?"

Jovinian's anger exploded. "Fellow!" he yelled, "Fellow? Do you call me fellow? Stand out of the way and let your Emperor in!"

The gatekeeper's eyes narrowed and the hand on Jovinian's chest began to press him backwards.

"Emperor? I see no Emperor here. All I see is a muddy, naked villain who's not quite right in the head. Clear off and stop making a nuisance of yourself."

Jovinian began to smell fear rising inside himself. Surely the man recognised his face?

"Look at me," he demanded. "Do you really not know your Emperor?"

"Of course I know him, you idiot. Why, it's only half an hour since he came riding in here on his beautiful chestnut stallion, collected my master and went away with him to the palace. Ay, and I'll tell you this as well, he was happy and singing and wearing his royal clothes, not naked and miserable like you, you wretch." And the hairy hand gave a final shove which sent Jovinian spinning backwards against the rough stone wall. The gate shut with a great slam and the Emperor was alone again.

Now what was he to do? Obviously someone who looked like him had stolen his clothes and horse, and was intent on taking his place as Emperor. Of course, riding the royal horse, wearing the royal robes he would get away with it for a time among those who didn't know him very well. But his friend should have known him well enough to spot

the impostor. Why then had he gone off riding with him – happy and singing, if the keeper were to be believed?

A cool shadow across the sun made Jovinian shiver as the full force of his predicament hit him. However one of his own Privy Councillors lived not far away, so Jovinian hopped and limped his way on torn feet until he came to the councillor's home. Again he hammered on the door and again he had to wait.

By this time he was fairly dirty. He had wiped his face with muddy hands, his body was mud-splashed and his legs and feet stained with the dust of the pathways. This time, too, he got a different reception. As soon as he started to explain who he was to the guard at the door he was arrested, dragged along cold stone corridors and flung still naked on the floor in front of his Privy Councillor, an old and wise knight. The knight stared at the trembling wretch who claimed to be the Emperor but he could see no resemblance at all to his beloved ruler.

"Impudent fool," he said, leaning back in his chair, "how dare you try to pass yourself off as the greatest man in the world? Here, guard, take this ruffian down to the cells, flog him soundly and then throw him out. He must be taught a lesson – we can't have idiots going around saying that they're emperors or the world will go mad."

So poor Jovinian found himself tumbled down smelly steps, thrown face down on to damp rushes, flogged soundly until his ribs and back burned like fire, and then flung back out of the gate into the roadway. He sobbed as he picked himself up. The sun was at its highest point and he cried aloud as he realised that it was only a few hours since he had climbed out of his silken sheets revelling in the thought that he was an emperor and a god. If this went on he would be dead before sunset.

There was only one place left to go. Even though it would take hours of walking, he must get home to his palace where his wife and family would recognise him, throw out the impostor and restore him to his own position.

It was the longest walk of Jovinian's life. He was spat at by jeering boys, followed by barking dogs, whipped by riders from whom he begged a lift. A very small child threw mud at him, and the only kindness he received was from a blind beggar who gave him a sack to cover his nakedness with. The sack was matted with dirt and scratched Jovinian's pink skin, but he was so grateful that he sobbed, the big tears making muddy channels down his dirt-encrusted face.

At last he reached his own home. Not daring to risk the main gate after his last two experiences, he slipped over the wall, and presented himself to the servant at the door of the dining-room in which, from the cheerful noises he could hear, the Empress was eating with the family.

The servant was very frightened by the sight of the half-naked madman and listened trembling to what he said before hurrying in to the Empress.

Inside the hall the Empress was dining with the one who had taken Jovinian's place. She listened to what the servant said while a look of surprise and pain passed over her face. Then, turning to her companion she touched his hand and said, "Dearest one, there is a man outside who is saying that he is you. It is most odd, for he has sent me all sorts of messages about things that only you and I know. What shall I do?"

"Fetch him in," said the one who was with her, and poor Jovinian was brought in. He looked with amazement at the man who wore his clothes, sitting by his wife and eating at his table. Yes, he did bear a superficial resemblance to himself, but surely she knew him? Crying out his story he rushed forward, but was caught and held back by the guards.

The one wearing the Emperor's clothes turned to the Empress. "Is this your husband?" he asked solemnly.

"How can you ask that, dearest one?" answered the

Empress, turning with a smile to the impostor. "Have we not been married for thirty years and have we not between us raised five lovely children? Surely you cannot imagine that I could believe that this wretch is anything like you?"

"Then take him away," said the false Emperor. "Tie him to the tail of a horse and run him out of town." And they went back to their meal while Jovinian once again suffered the pains and agonies of both physical and mental torture.

As night fell, Jovinian found himself near the bare cell of the priest who was his confessor. Painfully he staggered inside and knocked at the window of the cell.

"Who's there?" asked the Confessor from inside.

"The Emperor Jovinian."

The window flew open, his Confessor's amazed face appeared briefly and then the window was slammed shut.

He knocked again and heard his Confessor's frightened voice from behind the window: "Go away, madman. You are not the Emperor but some foul devil come to tempt me. Get thee behind me, Satan!"

The Emperor bowed his forehead against the window and sobbed. "At least let me make my confession," he said.

That brought a different answer. "Gladly, my son," said the priest, and the window opened again.

The Emperor began his confession by telling how he had got up saying to himself that he was a god, and how wrong he had been for he was after all only a poor, naked and very frightened man. Immediately the Confessor leaning forward in the darkness of the cell, recognised Jovinian, and came round to lead him inside where he tenderly washed him, fed him a simple meal and clothed him in poor but clean robes. Then he put the Emperor on his own donkey and led him back to the palace.

Strangely enough everyone they now met recognised the humble man on the donkey as the Emperor. Uproar broke out as they approached the palace gates and a messenger rushed in to where the Empress was sitting with the one who had taken Jovinian's place.

"Madam," he gasped. "We don't know what to do. Outside there is a man who appears to be the Emperor. Everyone swears that indeed it is he, but how can . . . ?" And he looked at the impostor.

"Come," said the impostor. He took the Empress by the hand and led her into the throne room where Jovinian stood waiting patiently. Then he went and stood by Jovinian and the two looked at her. "Now," said the impostor. "Which is your true husband?"

The poor woman did not know what to do or say, for the two were so alike, almost as if they were twins. She hesitated and then the one who had taken Jovinian's place spoke again.

"See," he said, pointing to Jovinian. "Here is your true husband and Emperor. But this very morning he became so proud of himself that he began to think that he was not only Emperor but also God. So God decided to punish him today by showing him that he is only a man and easily humbled. Now that he has repented of his foolish vanity, he is restored to his family and throne."

The court stared at the impostor and as they stared they saw a pale circle of light glowing round his head and his face began to shine with a beauty that was not of this world. He lifted both hands in blessing and spoke for the last time: "My work here is done now." And having spoken he disappeared, leaving behind him a wondering court, and a very humble Emperor.